DAXION

CONQUERED WORLD: BOOK FIVE

ELIN WYN

CLOCK
WALK
PUBLISHING

DAXION

It was my turn for night patrol inside the ship. I didn't mind, it gave me time to think about my family back home and wonder if they were still safe.

As the oldest of ten, it was my responsibility to look out for my siblings. When I joined the military, it was with their protection in mind.

Here, cut off from the rest of the war, I'd heard nothing. I could only hope.

The night shift went about their normal business on the second level, constantly maintaining the ship, trying to conduct repairs, and working alongside the humans.

Sakev's friends, Tona and Skit, were particularly enthusiastic about learning the ship's systems and proving their worth. I admired their tenacity to prove themselves, especially since Skit was so tiny compared to the rest of us.

Level three checked out. I double-checked all the doors that were supposed to be locked and verified everything was how it should be on level three. My teammates felt that this was extremely boring work, but that didn't matter.

It needed to be done.

The sweep of level four's living quarters showed nothing unusual, so back down to the main level with the refugee bay, infirmary, hangar bay, and several storage bays.

Where the sight of someone trying to hide behind a crate drew my attention.

I followed quietly, something that even Tu'ver would have found miraculous, considering my size. I couldn't tell if it was a man or a woman, but whoever it was, they were skinny and carrying a pack.

The form flitted from crate to crate, making its way towards the ship's exit door.

That was something I couldn't allow, not without General Rouhr's prior approval.

From behind a support pillar, I finally realized our potential runaway was a human woman.

Perhaps a less confrontational approach would be better.

As she neared the door, I stepped out from behind

the pillar and blocked the door, my arms folded across my chest.

I smiled down at her, but she still let out a small yelp.

"Good evening. Is there something that I might be able to help you with, Miss...?" I let the syllable hang with the idea that she would fill in her name.

She looked familiar, but I hadn't spent enough time around the refugees to easily tell them apart.

She looked up at me, anger a quick flash on her face as she dialed up a look of innocence, "Is there a problem?"

"I must apologize, but I can't let you leave the ship. It's far too dangerous to go out at night alone, Miss..." I tried to bait her, again, into giving me her name. She was so familiar...

She didn't bite. "You can't keep me here," she started, her voice obviously forced to be calm and level. "I'm not a prisoner. I have the right to leave anytime I want."

I nodded, "And I agree with you, Miss..."

She huffed a bit, "My name is Amira."

Of course. Jeneva's sister.

I nodded again, "And I am Daxion, of the first strike team. As I was saying, Miss Amira, I agree with you. You truly are not a prisoner, and you do have the ability to leave the ship, but I really must recommend you not leave at night...or alone."

She tried to say something, but I held up my hands to forestall her. "The situation is far too dangerous around here at night. I know that you've grown up on this world and know its creatures, but the Xathi are much different than anything else out there. They don't need light to find you. Please, for your own safety, stay on board."

"Are you really not hearing me right now? You can't keep me here. If I want to leave, I can leave," she insisted.

I decided to change tactics a bit. "If I may ask, why are you so insistent on leaving?"

She looked around and shuffled from foot to foot, then glared at me. "You're leaving anyway. Why should I stay?"

"Leave? What makes you believe that we will leave?"

With an exasperated sigh that seemed to indicate she was already tired of me and my questions, she snapped, "I heard your general plans to leave and close the rift, leaving Ankau to deal with the Xathi on our own. Someone even said you'd take us with you and leave the rest of the humans. How is that any better?"

I tried to steer her away from the door, but she resisted. I relented, but took a step back to better block the door. "There have been no official decisions made, it was only a possibility."

"It's still a possibility of you people running away

and leaving us to deal with those bugs. I will not leave my home," she said.

"If we were to leave, it would not be before giving the people of the planet the tools and knowledge needed to fight the Xathi or taking you with us."

I hesitated a second as I looked at her. If rumors were flying about the general's plans, it wouldn't hurt to try to set things straight. "To be honest, even if we decided to leave, General Rouhr would not do so without careful consideration. Additionally, the *Vengeance* still needs major repairs. Those will take a significant amount of time. We aren't going anywhere. We aren't leaving you."

That was reassuring, right?

Apparently not.

"It doesn't matter what you try to tell me, you're still thinking about leaving us to those monsters. The people deserve to know what's happening."

"Shouldn't you have all the information before you run off to tell people half of a story?"

That stopped her. She looked at me with a look that I interpreted as resignation.

I had won that point, I just hadn't known we were playing a game.

She tapped her foot on the deck and bit her lip in frustration, then decided to argue her point again. "You still can't keep me here. I have every right to leave."

"That you do," I said with a nod, "and I don't deny it. However, I would prefer not to arrest you."

She looked at me, bewilderment on her face and in her eyes. "What do you mean? Why would you arrest me?"

I pointed to the pack in her hand. "If you try to leave with those things, that would be considered theft. I would be forced to detain you and place you in the brig." I tried my best to hide my smile.

"You...you...how...why...but..." she stammered as she tried to find words.

"Inside that pack," I pointed at the pack on her shoulder, "I'm guessing you have some rations and a blaster. If you were smart, and I'm guessing you are, you also have a heat sensor in that pack, so you can see what's out there in the dark. Am I right?"

I folded my arms over my chest again.

She just nodded.

I didn't bother to hide my smile this time.

"Miss Amira, if you promise to go back to your room, at least for the night, and hand over the pack, I won't officially report this incident."

"Why not?" she asked, eyes narrowed.

"Because, you should be allowed to make your own decisions." She started to say something, but I kept talking, "If you wish to leave in the morning, I won't stop you."

After a few moments, she relented, handed over the pack, and stomped out of the hangar bay, presumably back to her room.

The final point went to me.

Right?

I watched her go. She wasn't the type to give up so easily.

How long would my victory last in the game I hadn't realized we were playing?

AMIRA

I woke to someone touching my shoulder.

Not yet awake, I rolled to the opposite side of my bed as fast as I could, almost falling off the bed completely. I grabbed for anything within reach, ready to use it as weapon, then the lights turned on.

"Jeneva!" I lowered the datapad I'd been reading late into the night and set it back down gently, as if to hide the fact that I'd been going to hurl it at my sister's head. To be fair, I didn't know it was my sister at the time.

"I thought waking you gently was a smart plan." Jeneva tried to smile. "I guess it backfired."

"Why are you waking me up in the first place?" I snapped. I closed my eyes and took a breath. I'd promised Jeneva I would work on my temper.

Not that she was keeping up with any of her promises.

This was the first time I'd seen her in a week, maybe longer. It was difficult to keep track of the days on the ship. There weren't a lot of windows, and even though the ship's lights dimmed for the night cycle, it didn't seem to make a difference in my brain.

"It's nearly midday." Jeneva blinked in surprise.

I was a late sleeper, it was true. After last night's misadventure, it was hours after midnight before I got back to my room.

"I waited in the refugee bay for hours, but you never showed up. I figured you were here."

"So, you just came in?" I asked. "Wait, how did you get in?"

"You never changed the code from when this was my room," Jeneva explained.

Jeneva now bunked with one of the strike team leaders, a Skotan named Vrehx. From what I could tell, he was great at what he did around the ship. Jeneva seemed happy too, happier than I ever remember her being.

The memories left a bitter taste in my mouth. When we were kids, I always remember Jeneva being unhappy or uncomfortable. No one in our family realized it at the time, but Jeneva could sense other people's feelings and moods.

When she was a kid, she couldn't control it. She was often in a great amount of pain, especially after our parents died, so she picked up and moved to the middle of the forest for over a decade. She left with no explanation and hardly a goodbye.

It wasn't until we were reunited on the *Vengeance* that I learned all of this.

"That doesn't give you the right to come and go as you please," I sniffed.

I'd been so angry at Jeneva for so long. If I'm being honest, I'm still angry. After I almost lost Jeneva for a second time, permanently, I swore I would try to build our relationship into what it was always supposed to be.

Which was harder than I'd hoped.

"And you don't have the right to sneak off the ship, the only safe place for miles, in the middle of the night," Jeneva shot back.

Now I knew why she was here.

"Did your boyfriend report me?" I glared.

Jeneva gave me a stern look. "No, Dax came to talk to me privately. Vrehx doesn't even know. I can't believe you would do something so risky and stupid!"

I wondered if Jeneva could feel what I was feeling now. "He had no right to go to you."

I couldn't think of anything else to say. Last night was not a shining moment of genius for me, but that didn't mean that Valorni could go around telling everyone.

It wasn't his business anyway, he'd done his job.

He kept me from doing something dangerous and stopped me from technically stealing, which I felt guilty about. There was no need for him to get involved any further.

"He's concerned for your safety," Jeneva argued.

"Well, that makes one person," I muttered.

"Excuse me?" Jeneva's eyes narrowed.

"Maybe if I had someone to talk to, like a *sister*, I wouldn't have tried to go through with such a stupid plan!" I exclaimed.

"You can always talk to me." Jeneva looked hurt.

"Only if I can find you. This ship is huge, Jeneva. I don't even know where you do your work. I never know when you go out into the field. I wouldn't know if something happened to you!"

"Of course, you would know." Jeneva spoke in a soft, gentle voice, as if I were a child. "Just like how I would know if something happened to you."

"Last week, I got sick and had to spend the night in the med bay with Dr. Parr." I folded my arms across my chest.

It wasn't anything serious. I just ate some alien food from the mess hall that I didn't know I was allergic to.

"Oh." Jeneva looked down at her feet. "Are you okay?"

"No, I died." I rolled my eyes.

"That isn't helping, Amira."

"What's not helping is you coming into my room in an attempt to be the sister you never were!" Tears welled in my eyes, and I looked away before Jeneva could see them.

I wanted this to be better.

I wanted **me** to be better.

I really did. But it was so hard to get out of my head, out of the past.

"I actually believed you were serious when you said you wanted to be more involved in my life. I guess that stopped when you met your alien soulmate."

I reacted badly the first day I was brought to the *Vengeance.* Jeneva had gone out of her way to rescue me and quite a few others. I was in shock, scared and surrounded by aliens and my long-lost sister.

I snapped. I yelled. I was mean.

It had earned me the title of "Jeneva's ungrateful little sister". I'd been able to drop that title since, but it still bothered me. Jeneva abandoned me for years, right after our parents died, but I'm the one who had to do all the work to fix our relationship because I'd had one bad day?

I'd done everything I could for people in the refugee bay. I helped Dr. Parr when she had her hands full. I helped Vidia teach lessons to the kids.

I even learned how to knit, so I could make blankets, hats, and socks! It was bitterly cold on the ship sometimes.

But it was never enough to make Jeneva pick me over Vrehx.

"I don't know what to do," Jeneva said so quietly, I could barely hear her. "You're angry with me when we don't spend time together, but when we do spend time together, you push me away. I don't know how to win."

"I get angry when you tell me you want things to be better and then don't follow through," I explained. "I push you away because I don't like feeling that you think you can show up whenever you want and expect things to be perfect."

"For the first time in a very long time, I have a real life. I can be around people and not feel like my head is going to explode. Can you understand that?" Jeneva pleaded.

"I can understand that it must have been horrible dealing with that growing up. I can understand how you thought the only solution was to live far away from people. But I don't understand why you shut me out of your life for ten years."

I didn't expect this. I wasn't prepared for this conversation. We hadn't talked about any of it since we were reunited.

"I couldn't bear to face you." Tears slipped down her cheeks. "I'd caused you so much pain."

"Did it ever occur to you that I would've been in much less pain if you'd just talked to me?" I pressed. "No, rather than own up to the damage you did, you decided to hide. That was a choice you made. I'd be able to forgive that, forgive *everything*, if you'd stop pretending that a few civilized conversations and a joke here and there are enough to fix what's broken."

"It's better than nothing." Jeneva didn't sound convinced by her own words. "I want to be the sister I should have been. I just don't know how." Understatement of the year.

"I'm not trying to hurt you, but the bottom line is that I don't trust you. It's hard for me to trust people. It takes time."

I didn't want to say it was her fault that I had trust issues. It might be true, but she was already hurting. I didn't need to make it worse.

"I understand," Jeneva nodded.

"I think it's best if you leave now. This was a lot. I think we both need some time."

I didn't want her to see how shaken I was. I was a

minute away from a complete breakdown. I didn't like anyone seeing me in that state.

"Okay." Her voice was weak with defeat as she slowly left the room. She paused at the doorway. "We'll talk later, okay?"

"Okay," I replied. I doubted that she would reach out to me later.

The door slid shut. I sat down on the bed, my legs shaking. My breathing was ragged as my throat felt tighter. I buried my face in my pillow and screamed.

After my parents died, I refused to let myself be swept away by grief. I had to keep pushing, so my life wouldn't fall apart.

I came up with a system for dealing with my emotions: The Five-Minute System. What the name lacked in creativity, it made up for in efficiency.

I set a timer for five minutes. In that five minutes, I could do whatever I needed to do: cry, scream, break something, whatever. But when the five minutes were up, I had to get it together.

I pulled up the timer on the mounted clock and started the countdown. I think I'd subconsciously trained myself to respond to the timer. Not even two seconds had passed, and I was on the deck, hugging my pillow and sobbing.

I refrained from breaking anything. Nothing here

actually belonged to me. When the timer was up, I calmed my shuddering breaths, washed my face, and started the day.

I needed to get out of that damn room.

DAXION

General Rouhr called all members of each strike team to his conference room for a meeting.

I arrived first, followed by Tu'ver, Vrehx, and eventually all the others, including Engineer Thribb. Axtin and Sakev were the last ones to arrive, laughing as they entered the room.

Rouhr started as they took their seats. "We have some serious things we need to talk about, and I want to start with the biggest issue on our plate." He paused, but I knew what he was going to say. We all did.

"The Xathi."

Since Sakev's return from Einhiv, there had been only one conversation swirling through the crew, apparently even bleeding over into the gossip of the refugees, judging by last night's interaction with Amira.

Should we find a way off the planet or continue to fight?

"We need to decide if we are going to stay on Ankau and continue to fight the Xathi, or if we're going to take the information we have already and try to get off-world," Rouhr said, echoing my thoughts.

Axtin was the first to respond. "Are we even able to leave? The *Vengeance* is still partially buried, and there aren't enough materials to fix her properly, even if we had everyone in Duvest working to get us the parts."

Thribb responded. "You are very correct, Axtin. The ship is in a very awkward predicament at the moment, as are we."

Thribb got up from his seat and walked over to the main screen. He brought up an inventory list and continued, "Our current situation does not afford us much opportunity for repairs. If we could conduct repairs without interruption, I estimate that it would take us just under a year to make the proper repairs needed for sustained space travel."

"How long just to get her in the air?" Axtin asked.

Thribb nodded at Axtin. "That would still take us several weeks, if we were uninterrupted. However, with the Xathi threat and the constant need for defense and patrols, we will need several months in order to get the *Vengeance* flying again."

"Then what is the point in trying to figure out if we

should stay or not?" Karzin asked. "Seems to me, our circumstances have already decided for us."

I had to agree with him to a degree. If the ship would be that difficult to repair, then all our efforts should be on stopping the Xathi.

However, there was something he had missed, and I wasn't the only one who saw it.

Takar spoke up. "Except we have a problem with our supplies, Karzin." He looked at his team leader. "We don't have the munitions needed to maintain a prolonged battle with the Xathi. Even if we were able to get weapons from the humans who are on our side, our own supplies are running low."

"What about those grenades Axtin and his human managed to create in Duvest?" Rokul, Takar's brother, asked.

Takar turned to look at his brother. "They are useful, but not fool-proof. Also, their range is limited, and their efficiency is dependent upon how many Xathi are in the immediate area."

Rouhr spoke up, taking control of the conversation. "Takar makes a valid point. We are limited with our supplies, and with more humans coming to stay every week, our stores are being taxed more than expected. We need to choose which direction is best for us. I see four possibilities, and one of them is not even a choice."

As he spoke, I agreed. Four options, none fabulous.

Choice one, we could continue to fight the Xathi and try to figure out what they were up to.

Choice two, we could concentrate our efforts on repairing the ship and leaving.

Choice three, we could split our concentration between ship repair and fighting, which is what we had been doing, with limited effectiveness.

Choice four? We could decide that we no longer stood a chance and conduct a final assault where we would most likely be destroyed.

"Sir?" Everyone turned their attention to me. I rarely ever spoke during meetings unless addressed first.

I didn't need to add extra words to the briefings. Usually things were pretty clear-cut.

But not anymore.

"What are we looking for exactly in regard to the Xathi?"

"May I?" Vrehx asked Rouhr.

Rouhr nodded and Vrehx got to his feet. He always talked better when he walked around.

"The Xathi are not acting as they normally do. When they attacked each of our planets, their method was to simply attack, destroy, and drain as many resources as possible, correct?"

Everyone in the room nodded in agreement.

It was how the Xathi had always worked. They

would swoop in, cause devastation, and while the Soldiers were fighting the planet's defenders, the Xathi Workers and Harvesters would denude the planet of whatever resources they could get.

It had happened on each of our homeworlds.

It wasn't something any of us would ever forget.

"They're not doing that here," Vrehx continued. "They've changed direction since we first landed, started an entirely new operation, as far as we can tell. They're working on creating the hybrids, taking over the human population."

He paused, scowling. "My original thought was they were using the humans to repair their own ship, but our patrols indicate that that's not happening, at least as far as we can see. The holes we blew in it," he said with a nod to Axtin, "are still there. They're using the humans for something else."

General Rouhr took the conversation back from Vrehx. "That is why we need to figure out what they're up to. This is a complete flip from what they normally do, and it has me concerned."

Thribb spoke up again, his distaste at his own words showing. "Sir," he said with a hint of respect in his voice, "I humbly disagree. As stated earlier, we are running low on munitions and other supplies. And despite the admirable showings of the humans that are working with us, we are limited in skilled warriors. I can't believe that I'm about to say this," and he shook his head as he did, "but I believe we should concentrate on fixing the ship and leaving this planet. It is better to live so we can fight again than to throw away our lives and never fight again."

It was an old Valorni saying, but every species I'd ever met had a variant of it.

Didn't mean I liked it.

"If the Xathi are acting differently, there must be a reason, and we need to know what that reason is. It could be the answer to defeating them," Takar argued.

Tu'ver nodded in agreement. "There is a chance that the humans either know something or are in possession of something that the Xathi want. That could be beneficial for us if we found it first."

Engineer Thribb spoke up. "That is a very logical argument, Tu'ver. However, our current limited supplies do not afford us an opportunity to conduct such an investigation. Our best course of action is to repair the ship as best as possible, then make our way off the planet and back through the rift."

Rouhr stood, silencing the rest of us. "Let me pose this question to everyone. If we were to leave the planet and escape through the rift, how would your consciences handle the idea of abandoning the humans here? Humans whom we have become friends with, might I remind you."

The room was quiet. Each team had their own human contacts around the continent and had made friends with several of the humans on board. Tona and Skit, as well as other guards and soldiers, had already made an impression on each team, as had the women who had become part of our crew's families.

Evie was invaluable in the infirmary and in her study of the hybrids. Jeneva had taught each of us how to survive the wilderness where even the trees tried to kill you. Mariella and Leena worked in the lab, finding new ways to deal with the Xathi and how to modify the neuro-weapons we had invented.

Rouhr broke the silence. "I, in good conscience, cannot fathom the idea of leaving behind so many people to try to defend themselves against an enemy that even we, with superior technology, struggle with. Even if it is the logical decision," he said with a nod to Thribb, "I believe that it is the wrong decision. But... that is my belief. Each of you have laid out your thoughts, at least most of you have, and you all make compelling cases. We just need to figure out our plan of action. We can't split our concentrations anymore. It's holding us back and hurting us. We need to choose."

I already knew my choice. I wanted to know why the Xathi were behaving as they were. If there was something in the human mind, or whatever, that could benefit all of us, I wanted to know what it was.

Then, something occurred to me. "Sir? What about the *Aurora?*"

Rouhr looked at me and smiled. "According to Fen's latest reports, the Xathi population in the Kangefi wetlands is negligible. She estimates single digits and believes it's because there are no humans left in the wetlands, so they've left the *Aurora* alone. Any that were there have either been infected or escaped. Actually, hold on."

The general looked down at his tablet, then smiled as he looked up. "Some good news, for a change. Fen and her people have agreed to share whatever resources they can spare."

A slight relaxing of tension rolled around the table. It meant that we had a little more to help keep ourselves going, no matter what decision we made.

At least for a little while.

He looked at Vrehx. "I need you and your team to go back to the *Aurora* and coordinate with Fen to run a proper inventory. Find out what kind of resources they have and what we can use."

"Aye, sir." Vrehx responded.

"Sir?" I asked.

"You're mighty talkative today, Dax." Rouhr smiled. "What is it?"

"I'd like to include Amira on this trip, if you

wouldn't mind." It was a calculated gamble, but I had to ask.

"Why?"

"She's deeply embedded with the refugee population. We know how quickly rumors can fly when a crew is under tension. If the humans don't have information, they'll jump to conclusions. It's far too likely those conclusions could be an additional problem we'll need to attend to."

I shot a sly look towards my strike captain. "Besides, if Amira can participate and show her worth, that will make Jeneva happier, which will make Vrehx happier, which makes all of us happier. Sir."

From the corner of my eye, I could see Vrehx's scowl.

Rouhr grinned. "I understand. Very well, take her along."

This was going to be interesting.

AMIRA

I still felt rotten about what had happened with Jeneva that morning. I was sure Jeneva felt bad about it, too, which is why I was so surprised to see her rushing across the refugee bay with an excited look in her eyes.

When she approached the table where I sat, she said an awkward hello to my friends. I doubted that she knew their names.

"Amira, I have some good news!" Jeneva said cheerfully. "Strike team one is heading over to the *Aurora* in a little while, and Dax recommended that you go along."

My face fell. I tried to hide it, but I knew Jeneva noticed. "I don't understand."

"Dax? The Valorni who caught you last night," Jeneva prompted.

I stole a quick glance at my friends, all of whom were giving me a confused look. I hadn't exactly told them I was planning on sneaking off the ship.

"I know who you're talking about. I just don't understand why he'd recommend me, or why he'd think I'd want to go." As soon as the words left my mouth, I realized I should've phrased them better.

"You were so desperate to get off the ship last night. Dax thought this would be a good chance for you to get out for a little bit. It's not like he's asking you to work." Jeneva crossed her arms over her chest.

First, Dax covered for me after my poorly executed escape plan. Now, he was offering to take me off the ship?

I didn't understand it. We didn't know each other. He had no reason to go out of his way to do something nice for me, as misguided as it was.

"Are you going?" I asked.

"No, I've got to find a few plant samples for Leena's lab."

Now I was even more confused. "So, you want me to go off with a team of aliens I don't know, and you're not even going to be there?"

"This is a chance for you to get to know them! They're a big part of my life now. And you get what you want, to get off the ship for a little while. I don't understand why you aren't happy about this."

I believed her. Jeneva genuinely didn't understand why I didn't want to go.

"It never occurred to you to *ask* me?"

Her shoulders slumped. "There's no pleasing you, is there? This morning, you were upset because I don't include you in my life. Now you're upset because I *am* including you in my life?"

I wanted to argue. I *really* wanted to argue. But Jeneva looked so bewildered that this didn't go like she imagined it was going to go.

She was trying, in her own way.

I needed to try, too.

"Okay, you're right." I sighed. "I'm sorry. I'll go with Dax to the *Aurora*. I'm sure you're right. It'll do me some good to get off the ship for a while."

"You're going to enjoy yourself! I know you will." Jeneva was practically bouncing. "I've got to get back to work. Head over to the docking bay when you're ready. They're planning to leave in an hour or so."

"I'll be sure to do that." My smile looked more like a grimace.

Jeneva gave me a suspicious look. "If you don't show up, Dax is just going to track you down."

"He's really good at that, apparently."

Jeneva smiled and rolled her eyes before leaving the refugee bay.

"You're not seriously going to go, right?" Ren, one of the first people I'd befriended on the *Vengeance*, grabbed my arm.

I shifted out of his grip. He was a touchy-feely person.

I very much was not. Somehow, he never caught on.

Ren and I had both lived in Kaster. He worked as a programmer while I was finishing school, but we hadn't met until we got here.

"I think I should," I confessed.

I told Jeneva I would. If Dax did come find me, it would be easy for me to tell him off. But then he'd tell Jeneva I didn't go, and her feelings would be hurt.

As annoyed as I was that she didn't ask me about any of this, I didn't want to hurt her feelings. I'd done that enough this morning.

"It would make me feel better if you stayed behind," Ren admitted. "You said yourself that you don't know these aliens."

"Well, one of them is in love with my sister, so I can't imagine he'll be any trouble," I reasoned. "And one of them could've been a real asshole yesterday, but he wasn't. I don't think I have anything to worry about on that end."

"But they're still aliens," Ren pressed.

He'd been doing this more often lately. I'll admit that when I first got here, I didn't trust anyone with red, gray, or green skin. I was outright mean to some of them for no real reason.

Now I knew that the Skotans, K'ver, and Valorni wanted to help us. They didn't have to take us in, they didn't have to feed us, and they certainly didn't have to protect us.

I trusted them as much as I trusted anyone else.

Which wasn't much, but at least I was being consistent.

At least I was taking steps in the right direction.

Ren seemed to be going backwards.

"If these aliens were going to do something bad to us, they would've done it by now. It would mean a lot to Jeneva if I went, so I'm going. There's nothing more to it than that, so you don't have to get all up in arms about it."

I pushed away from the table before Ren could say another word.

I'd never been to the docking bay before. It took me nearly half an hour to find it.

I was one of the last people to get fitted for a neurotranslator. I'd refused when they were first offered to us. Now I regretted not getting one sooner.

It was nice to be able to understand everyone,

regardless of language. I still struggled with reading the alien languages, though.

Jeneva had promised to help me but she never made the time...I caught myself. Maybe I shouldn't blame her for that. Other people could help.

"Amira," Dax said formally. "You made it." He beamed when I arrived, before turning to Axtin. "Pay up, Axtin."

A second burly Valorni tossed Dax a couple of currency chips.

"It's easy earnings," Dax said when he noticed my surprised expression.

"Amira." Vrehx strode around the outside of the shuttle I assumed we'd be using. "You're looking well." His speech was strained. I decided to give him a break.

"Jeneva lectured you about being nice to me, didn't she?" I asked with a wry smile.

Vrehx let out a short, relieved breath. "That she did."

"Don't worry, I won't bite."

I ended up wedged between Dax and Axtin, absolute giants. I tucked my arms and legs in as close as possible to avoid getting bumped as the ship moved out of the dock.

Craning my neck, I peered out the window, but I couldn't see much other than the tops of the tallest trees.

"Are you a student of the plants and animals like your sister is?" Dax asked.

"Not really," I replied. I should say something back. Maybe ask a question about his life?

I hated small talk. I was terrible at it. I could never find the balance between saying too much and saying too little.

I could say that Jeneva was never interested in plants or animals until she had to depend on them for a living. It was incredibly clever of her, and I don't think I could've done that if I'd been in the same situation. But was that something to bring up with a stranger?

Damn it.

"What did you do for a living before all this happened?" Another question with an unclear answer.

I could just say archaeology. That's what I went to school for, but it wasn't exactly an explosive field on this planet.

I certainly hadn't made a living doing it. I worked in the only decent store in Kaster until the Xathi attacked. It paid the bills.

"Archaeology," I mumbled.

"I suppose that's interesting," Dax pressed. He looked out the window at the expanse of forest. "I would guess there are many secrets to dig up in there."

"Good luck digging up anything with those giant trees walking around," Axtin chimed in.

It was a fair point. If I ever were to set up a proper excavation site somewhere in the forest, there's no way I'd be able to protect it from any of the hostile creatures roaming about.

"Hang on, I've got movement down below." Dax's tone changed completely. He shifted to get a better view, bumping my shoulder with his backside.

"What do you see?" Vrehx asked from the row of seats in front of us.

"Not sure, but it's big. It's knocking over trees as it moves. Can you take us down closer, Tu'ver?"

I braced myself as the craft dipped and banked.

"Skrell, it's the Xathi. Hundreds of them. And hybrids, too. They look like they're heading right for the *Vengeance*."

My stomach dropped.

When the Xathi had moved in on my hometown, there were only a dozen of them, if that. One dozen was all it took to overrun Kaster. I couldn't imagine what hundreds of those monsters were capable of.

"I'll get Rouhr on the radio. Tu'ver, get us back to the ship as fast as you can," Vrehx ordered.

The trees outside were a blur as we sped back to the *Vengeance*.

Panic reared up inside me, but I suppressed it. Panicking lead to stupidity.

In this case, stupidity would lead to death.

And I wasn't ready to give up on whatever tenuous friendship Jeneva and I were figuring out.

Daxion's large hand rested lightly on my knee. Just for a moment, the barest touch of comfort, safety.

"So much for getting off the *Vengeance* for a day," Dax said with false cheerfulness.

Despite myself, a tight grin twisted my lips.

But the knot in my stomach only tightened at what lay in store for us.

DAXION

The Xathi came in hard and fast, and our pilot spun us around with impressive agility. Strike teams two and three were already engaged as we flew in over their heads back into the docking bay.

The pilot landed us quickly, the shuttle doors opening before we touched down.

Axtin and Sakev were the first off the shuttle, charging to take defensive positions. Tu'ver was next as Vrehx and I brought up the rear. Out of the corner of my eye, I saw Amira take off to the refugee bay. I watched, just a bit longer than I should have, before the battle outside claimed all my attention.

Karzin and his team had spread themselves out to the left, while Sk'lar had his team covering the bay doors. Vrehx ordered us to the right where another wave of Xathi was coming out of the trees.

"How the hell did they find us?" Sk'lar yelled as we ran behind them. He fired off a shot from his massive rifle, taking down two Xathi with a single shot.

"I don't know!" Vrehx fired off a shot of his own.

The Xathi were rabid and careless in their attack. They rushed in without even trying to avoid our fire.

Blue Soldiers, black Hunters, and even green Workers flowed out of the forest. They ran over and around one another as they came at us.

Axtin tossed his rifles to some of the human guards and drew his hammer from his back.

I loaded my crossbow and fired, catching a Hunter just behind a shoulder joint. It fell over, tripping up three Soldiers running behind it.

"What's the plan?" I shouted at Vrehx.

He waved me off as he fired, then put his hand to his ear. I figured he was getting information from inside, so I concentrated on the Xathi.

Axtin was already engaged with them in hand-to-claw combat, as was Sakev with his swords. Tu'ver had somehow managed to climb up the side of the *Vengeance* and found himself a perch from which to shoot. He fired off shot after shot, rarely missing his target.

I managed three more shots with my crossbow

before I slung it over my shoulder and took out two bolts from my quiver. Luckily, I had made sure my bolts were very heavy and strong, so I could use them in up-close combat as well. I charged in and engaged a Hunter.

Despite it being more agile than the other Xathi, I was able to get a bolt into one of the soft spots at the bottom of its jaw. It thrashed and shook as it fell to the ground. I kicked it to the side and moved on to another.

A Soldier managed a cut to my back before Tu'ver shot it down. I kicked another's leg, snapping it off, then stabbed it in the back of the head as it stumbled. I left the bolt behind, grabbed another from my quiver, and blocked a Hunter's pincers from crushing my head.

I roared in its face and ripped the pincers off. I clubbed it over the head with its own pincer, then stabbed it down into the crack I had made in its head.

Something tackled me and I felt a horrific pain in the back of my right leg. Looking back, a Worker gnawed mindlessly on my calf.

I reached down and smacked it away, rolled over, kicked it, then flung myself forward and stabbed down with my bolts.

Throwing the spasming body at a pair of Hunters coming for me, the impact shattered the Worker and broke the legs of the Hunters. Four rounds zinged passed my head and struck the Hunters, killing them.

I looked back to see Vrehx and one of the humans, Skit I think, nod at me. I pulled back towards them, my leg bleeding, and ducked behind a log that still lay close to the ship.

As I worked on bandaging myself, I looked at Vrehx. "What's the plan?"

"We hold them off until the auto-defenses finish coming online, then we pull back and pick them off. Too much power was diverted to recycling, it's taking too long to switch. How's the leg?"

He jutted his chin at me. He fired off another shot, cursed, then fired another round.

Skit ran off to help at the bay doors.

"Leg's fine, just a small scratch." I ripped my shirt and wrapped it tightly around my wound. "Any idea how they found us?"

"No, but it was only a matter of time. Are you good?"

At my nod, he got to his feet and ran over towards the right, firing as he went. Several Hunters had made it past Axtin and Sakev and were making their way towards a small line of humans who were already busy with several Workers.

I caught sight of one of the crews and yelled at him to bring me my big gun, but he told me that one of the brothers was using it.

Skrell!

I unslung my crossbow again and began firing. As my quiver ran low, I grabbed some nearby branches and leaves and packed them into the quiver.

I was particularly proud of my invention. Sakev and I had managed to miniaturize an organic transmogrifier and reprogram it. Now my quiver was able to take any organic material and turn it into new bolts for my crossbow.

Not instantaneously, but better than running out of ammo.

I fired off my last three bolts as my quiver worked, then limped my way over to the hangar bay. I called for a weapon and was given a rifle. I turned and fired on a Soldier who was about to attack Sakev from behind, then fired into a pack of Hunters.

I was proud to see several humans fighting alongside and happy that someone had remembered to bring some of the neurogrenades to use.

Small explosions erupted all around the ship as grenades were thrown, each followed by rapid fire. I could hear the whine of my big gun coming from the left as Takar and Rokul's yells of joy accompanied it.

I heard the ship's defenses come online and felt the slight vibration of the guns aligning, then they began firing. Our people retreated as the ground erupted all around them from the ship's gunfire.

"INSIDE!" Vrehx's orders echoed down the line and around the ship.

Evie, who was checking on the wounded in the bay, looked at me with a raised eyebrow. I waved her off and turned to the opening.

Axtin was scratched up, Sakev had a small cut to his head, and Tu'ver was untouched. The members of the other strike teams had similar small injuries, and most of the humans seemed okay.

"Report!" Vrehx called out.

A Skotan crew member sitting against a crate with his arm in a sling answered. "They just came out of the trees like wildfire, sir. At least four humans and two crew members dead, another six or so injured."

Vrehx nodded. The other two teams were lined along the bay doors, firing on the Xathi that made it past the ship's defenses. He looked at us.

"Sakev, get yourself cleaned up. You're bleeding. The rest of us will reload and..." Vrehx stopped and put his hand to his ear. The curse he muttered made my eyes go wide. "Nearly two dozen Hunters and Soldiers have gotten past the defenses and are making their way into the ship through some of our damaged areas. Workers tunneled under. They're inside the ship."

To verify his words, klaxon alarms sounded throughout the hangar bay. A shout from Karzin turned our attention to the bay doors, where a wave of blue and black Xathi rumbled towards us, ignoring the gunfire cutting them down.

We rushed over and opened fire. It felt hopeless, to see them coming at us with sheer disregard for everything, but we didn't give up.

I took a comm unit from a nearby guard and listened to reports from around the ship. The Xathi were on board, and General Rouhr was calling for an evacuation.

Vrehx glanced at me as I glanced at him.

We were abandoning the ship?

He motioned for me to get inside. I knew he wanted me to help get everyone onto the shuttles. I fired off a few more shots, handed my rifle off to a nearby human, and ran back in.

At the back of the hangar bay, I caught a flash of Amira, working with some of the other women.

I grabbed a few of the injured guards, reloaded their weapons, and helped them over towards the inner doors.

"If you see anything with more than two legs, shoot it," I ordered them.

Amira, Vidia, and Evie directed the humans towards the shuttles. They were doing what they could to keep everyone calm, a difficult thing to do under these circumstances.

The humans made me proud. Most of them were

listening and heading towards the shuttles with little in the way of panic, although they were unable to hide their fear.

Gunfire came from the bowels of the ship, and that scared me more than anything else had scared me before. The idea that our ship, our home, *my* home was invaded…again…brought back memories that I never wanted to recall.

I forced my thoughts back to the present and looked at Amira. After a quick check with the guards, I hurried over to her.

"Why are you still here?"

AMIRA

"*Xathi incoming. Xathi incoming.*" Vrehx's staticky voice hissed through Dax's radio.

"Shit!" We'd gotten most of the people out of the docking bay and onto some form of transport, but we were running out of space.

I grabbed the arm of a panicking girl and pulled her close. "There's room here, sit on his lap!" I pointed to the scrapper parked in front of me.

"I'm not sitting on a stranger's lap!" the girl shrieked.

"Lady, it's either this or death. Make a decision!" I watched the gravity of the situation settle over the girl. She practically leaped into the scrapper.

"It's time for you to get out of here!" Dax shouted over the din.

The fighting was getting closer. I could hear them now.

"Not a chance!" I shouted back. "I didn't see Jeneva. I'm not leaving until I know she made it out."

The door to the docking bay burst open as the Xathi pushed their way through. A chill shot down my spine when I heard them clicking and shrieking to one another.

I hadn't heard that since they attacked Kaster, but it's not something I'd ever forget.

"Are you using that?" I pointed to the blaster strapped to Dax's thigh.

"Not at the moment but—"

"Great! I'm going to borrow it." I yanked it out of its sheath and took aim.

"Do you even know how to shoot?" Dax asked.

"Why would I have taken it if I didn't?"

Dax paused, unsure of how to respond. "Just…aim for the leg joints."

I raised the blaster and fired. Several yards away, a Xathi's leg joint exploded.

"Nice shot."

"Thanks! Now go fight the bad guys. I'll be fine here." I took aim again.

"Keep as much distance between yourself and the fighting as possible. And if you see a spot on a shuttle, take it!" He paused as if he'd say something else, but charged back into the battle, using his special bolts like they were short swords.

He jabbed the barbed head into the joint of a Xathi. When he yanked it out, the entire leg came with it.

The Xathi seemed more concerned with reaching the shuttles and troop carriers than killing the crew.

Interesting, but not information I could do anything about.

I hid behind a row of storage crates and fired at any Xathi that made it through the line of soldiers and crew members.

I didn't kill any, but I slowed them down enough for someone else to finish the job. As strange as it was for me to admit it, I was enjoying myself.

I felt like I was helping.

It wasn't long before Dax broke away from the combat to find me.

"It's not looking good." He was out of breath. "We're planning on retreating. You need to leave, now!"

"I don't know where Jeneva is!" I argued.

"I'll look for her, I promise," Dax assured me. "Vrehx is here, too. You know he wouldn't let anything happen to her. But you need to go."

Dax lifted me off the ground. To his credit, he tried to hold me comfortably, but I was kicking and thrashing like a maniac.

He threw me into one of the evac shuttles as gently

as someone can throw another person in the middle of a warzone.

"Get them out of here!" he ordered the pilot.

The doors slid shut before I could do anything about it. I banged on the shuttle door, as if that would do anything. The last thing I saw was another wave of Xathi flood the docking bay.

The ride to the *Aurora* was riddled with anxiety.

Jeneva had to be there, she simply had to. She was not stupid. She'd lived in the forest for so long, she would've heard the Xathi coming long before anyone else did.

She'd be there.

Everything would be okay.

If I repeated it enough times, would it be true?

When the carrier landed, I was the first one out. I hit the ground running, trying my best not to collide with anyone.

People were in shock. Some had minor injuries, but no one looked too poorly.

I couldn't help but notice that there were less people than there had been before. I tried not to think about it.

"Jeneva!" I doubted she could hear me over the chaos. I stopped moving briefly to catch my breath and orient myself. A hand touched my shoulder.

"Amira." It was Jeneva. I hugged her tightly.

"What's all over you?" I gasped. I was now covered in something dark, thick, and slimy.

"I was out in the field when the Xathi showed up. I hid in a mud patch so they wouldn't find me." She laughed nervously.

"Good thinking." I tried not to wrinkle my nose. The mud smelled horrible. "Are you sure it was mud?"

"No, but I'm not going to think about it too much," Jeneva winced.

Our laughter was hesitant and uneasy at first. It felt wrong to laugh after something so horrible had happened, but we couldn't hold it in. We were soon cackling like mad women.

"I was so worried!" I wiped a tear from my eye, no doubt smearing mud across my face in the process. "Dax had to throw me onto a carrier because I wouldn't stop looking for you."

"I was worried, too." Jeneva tried to wipe the mud off my face, with little success. I think she just made it worse. "When you weren't here when I arrived, I was beside myself. As soon as Vrehx gets here, I'm going to ask him for personal radios for us."

"Not a bad idea. He'll be okay though, right?" I looked in the direction of the *Vengeance.*

"He's tougher than he looks." Jeneva winked.

"All of them look pretty damn tough to begin with."

I turned my gaze to the *Aurora.* It was larger than

the *Vengeance* and, aside from the gash in the hull, was gorgeous.

"Are you going to sneak off this ship, too?" Jeneva's tone was light, but I could hear the seriousness behind her words.

I chewed on my bottom lip. "You accepted all of this so easily. I wasn't ready to let go of how the world used to be. But I realize how stupid that was. This world, our world, has changed so much, and it's going to keep changing whether I want it to or not. Getting away from ships and aliens won't change the fact that I'll still be surrounded by the dangers of the Xathi. There's no going back, so I won't keep trying."

"That takes a weight of my chest to hear you say that." Jeneva sighed and pulled me in for another hug.

I rested my head on her shoulder, not caring about the mud anymore. I let my gaze roam over the forest. It was then that something caught my eye over the tree line.

"Look!" I pulled away from Jeneva and pointed. Quickly moving towards us was a small fleet comprised of whatever transport units from the *Vengeance* that hadn't been used for evacuation.

"That must be them!" Jeneva grabbed my hand and took off running. Her legs were longer than mine. I struggled to keep up.

A few other human women were waiting near

where the fleet was going to land. Mariella and her sister, Leena, grasped hands. Dr. Parr nervously twirled a lock of hair that had escaped her ponytail.

One by one, the units landed, and crew members piled out. Some were wounded, some were completely unscathed. Again, fewer than there had been before.

I spotted Vrehx at the same moment Jeneva did. She gave me an eager but uncertain look.

"Go get your alien," I snorted, pushing her in his direction. She mouthed a thank you before hurling herself into his arms.

I spotted Dax shortly after. Aside from a few scratches, he didn't look any worse for wear. I made my way over to him. He smiled when he saw me.

"I'd almost wagered Axtin that you found a way to jump off the evac shuttle, but there wasn't time," he jested. "Good thing I didn't. I would've lost that bet. How's Jeneva?"

I looked over my shoulder to where she was still wrapped up with Vrehx.

"I think she's going to be just fine." I smirked. "Glad you made it back in one piece."

"Same to you," he nodded.

We stood quietly for a moment, but the silence soon turned awkward.

"Look," I started, "it means a lot that you took the

time to help people get out. A lot of the people here are here because of you."

"All part of the job." He shrugged, but I saw the smile pulling at the corners of his mouth.

"And I'm sorry that I wasn't the nicest person when we first met," I added quickly. Heat flooded my face. I was terrible with apologies.

"Apology accepted. Though I'd argue you have nothing to apologize for. Aside from the attempted theft, you weren't a complete nightmare."

"I can't tell if that was a compliment or not." I laughed.

"It was a compliment, just a poorly worded one," Dax admitted. "Let me try again. You're a skrell of a good shot with a blaster. How'd you learn?"

"Thank you." I nodded. "I took it up as a hobby a few years back. It was a great way for me to deal with anger."

I started practicing when my parents died. It was good for the stress.

"That's quite impressive and a little concerning. But a good mix." He chuckled.

"I try to keep it versatile."

"Since your skills were so helpful back on the *Vengeance*," Dax started, "I think you should come to the regroup meeting General Rouhr called."

I wasn't expecting that.

Jeneva went to those meetings all the time. I'd always been curious as to what everyone was talking about, though I'd never admit it. If Ren knew, he'd freak out.

"Are you sure that's okay?" I didn't know General Rouhr at all. Jeneva had told me he's nice, but I didn't want to get on his bad side.

"It is. The large number of relationships you have established with the human refugee population will be helpful in any discussion. General Rouhr likes meeting helpful people, especially now when it's so important for everyone to work together."

A little thrill ran through me when Dax called me helpful.

"All right, you've convinced me!" I put my hands up in mock surrender. "I'd be happy to go."

The smile of pleasure on his face sent another jolt through me.

What the hell was this?

DAXION

The trip to the *Aurora* had been bad.

Many of the refugees were scared, and not every crew member was a soldier, so not all of them were able to deal well with what happened, either. I still had my comm device on, so I heard the reports.

When we arrived at the *Aurora*, out in the Kangeti wetlands, things were a bit chaotic as we did our best to get everyone on board and organized. Many of the humans looked at Fen's people with caution. Many of them had not seen Fen when Sakev brought her on board, and despite the speed of gossip, not everyone was prepared for an actual meeting.

It was hours before General Rouhr called together an emergency meeting. Fen had to open a wall between two rooms to accommodate everyone who wanted to be present.

The wall was a magnificent piece of engineering. It simply shrunk within itself as she pushed it off to the side, emphasizing the two small windows that looked outside.

Each member of the strike teams was there, some of them still working on bandaging themselves. Vidia, the human leader, was there, as were Evie, Jeneva, and Amira. Fen and two of her Urai kin were there as well.

Rounding out our two dozen participants was one of the engineers. Thribb had been injured and was too incapacitated to attend.

I looked around the room. No one was calm. The quiet conversations between different groups were heated, or frightened, or, in the case of the Urai, robotic.

Fen and several of her kind had outfitted themselves with a small speech device that they wore around their necks. When they touched it, their thoughts were transmitted out as words, making it easier to hold a conversation for those of us who were still bothered with the idea of them being in our heads.

I wasn't as suspicious of them as my other Valorni brethren were, but I wasn't volunteering for long conversations, either.

"Can anyone tell me what just happened?" Rouhr

DAXION   59

asked. His question quieted everyone in the room. "We always knew it would be a matter of time before they found us, but this was coordinated. They knew exactly how to get in and how to draw our attention."

"I don't know, sir," Sk'lar answered. "We haven't had an opportunity to debrief everyone yet."

The general nodded, but it was a nod of resignation more than of acceptance. With a deep breath, he looked around the room.

"Anyone else? Anyone?" Then he looked at Evie. "Evie, you've had a chance to go through the human refugees since your return. Is anyone showing signs of infection?"

Evie shook her head. "No, sir. From what I was able to see, and from what Fen's people told me, everyone aboard was clean. No signs of hybridism on anyone."

"Then how did they find us?" Rouhr asked, a definitive growl entering his voice. It was easy to guess that he didn't want hybridism to be the reason, but it frustrated him that they had no answer yet.

Any of the alternatives would be just as bad, if not worse.

Vidia, sitting next to the general, placed her hand on his hand for a moment before pulling it back.

That was new.

And very interesting.

Then she spoke, and my attention snapped back.

"When we were fleeing after the Xathi attack on Fraga, someone sold us out. It led to the capture of us all. He was under the impression that the Xathi would spare him if he gave us up. That might have happened here. He might not have been the only one with that idea."

Her voice had been calm, which made her words even more devastating to hear. We knew that there were humans who hated us simply because we were different, but we never, or at least I never, thought that any of them would betray us to a common enemy.

"So, you mean that someone told them, and that someone could still be with us?" Sakev asked. He didn't look happy.

Vidia nodded sadly.

Rouhr didn't look very happy, either. "Okay, with that idea in mind, how do we go about protecting the *Aurora*?"

Fen put her hand on her speech pad and answered. "There is little to fear here, my friends. The *Aurora* is protected by a sonic barrier that disrupts the Xathi mental connection to one another. Without that connection, the Xathi are aimless, useless creatures."

Sk'lar looked at Fen and challenged her answer. "Wait a moment. If your little sonic shield thing keeps the Xathi away, then what about that video we found where a queen drove everyone insane, and your people decided to open the airlock and die instead of staying under her control?"

Fen turned to look at Sk'lar, her eyes growing a bit lighter in color. "You make a fair point, friend Sk'lar. I have reviewed the recordings of my brethren and have determined that the sonic barrier was down when they were attacked."

"Why would they do such a thing?" Sk'lar narrowed his eyes, apparently as confused as the rest of us.

"During space flight, there are times when the barrier must be deactivated in order to recharge. If the Xathi queen had kept an unrelenting attack on the ship, her poisonous thoughts could have slipped through during one of those times." Her eyes closed, her strange face showing what might have been sorrow. "Just one weak mind would have been enough. Her victim could have found ways to keep the barrier down until more were infected."

I watched Sk'lar think about her answer, then he nodded and sat back in his chair, nursing his shoulder. His team had taken the brunt of the initial attack, and Sk'lar had come out of it the best, with a dislocated shoulder.

Jalok and Cazak, the two Skotans on his team, had each broken an arm and received numerous cuts and bites. Tyehn, my cousin through marriage, had bandages on his head, chest, and both arms, and had his right leg in a temporary air-cast, but had insisted on being part of this. Navat had a bandaged rib cage.

None of us had come away from the battle unscathed.

I turned my attention back to the conversation. Amira had asked Fen her about thoughts regarding the Xathi tactics.

"It is my belief that the Xathi are acting in such a way as an attempt at some form of psychological indoctrination. They are trying to incorporate the human mind into their collective hive-mind to increase their own capabilities."

That was a frightening thought.

Fen continued with her answer. "Of course, there is another belief amongst my fellow Urai that there could be something within the human mind, or something within human possession, that the Xathi are looking for, something that may give them a sizeable advantage in their quest."

I could see that Amira wanted to ask more questions, but Rouhr politely interrupted.

"There are some important matters that we need to address right now. I want to find out what the Xathi are up to as much as you do, I promise, but we need to ensure our safety for the moment." He turned to Fen and began talking to her.

The conversation revolved around the defense of

the *Aurora,* and possibly the island itself. While Fen and the Urai were confident in the sonic barrier, Rouhr was curious about other defenses.

Each team leader participated in the conversation, coming up with a plan for defenses in case the Xathi made their way here. The *Aurora* was unable to fly, but repairs were already underway. In the short time since Fen had awakened the other survivors who had been in stasis, they had already gotten many major systems back online: life support, food production, the sonic barrier, proximity sensors, and the ship's medical library.

During the next two hours, plans for defense, medical care, and living arrangements were made. Vidia wanted to try to integrate the human population with the rest of the crew in order to help foster better communication and to help those who were still wary of us become better used to us. And the general felt that it was a good idea.

Fen volunteered several levels of the ship as living quarters and had announced that her people had already created maps with directions for everyone to access, as well as easy access to several things aboard the ship to help. Obviously, more sensitive systems were restricted, but the Urai wanted everyone to feel as comfortable as they could aboard their ship.

The *Aurora* certainly was different from the

Vengeance. While the *Vengeance* was a military vessel with clean halls and little to no accoutrements of comfort, the *Aurora* was the complete opposite. The halls were a calming color, the seats in the conference room were plush and comfortable, and even the floors were covered in a soft material that seemed to lighten the step.

The med bay aboard our ship was state-of-the-art, or so we had thought. The med bay aboard this ship, the *three* med bays aboard this ship, made ours look like a warehouse filled with terrible beds. Everything that the *Vengeance* was, the *Aurora* was better.

"Any idea of how long the repairs may take?" the engineer asked. She was one of Thribb's people, so I was sure that whatever Thribb thought, she'd echo.

One of the other Urai answered, his robotic voice deeper than Fen's. It made me wonder if the speech pads were programmed for different voices, or if his thoughts were just deeper in volume than hers. "Our own numbers have been significantly reduced due to the attack. With the number of Urai currently on board, it will take several of your weeks to get the structural repairs finished, then we can move on to the engines, which will take several weeks more."

"Could you teach us about your technology?" The engineer's idea was obvious. If the Urai taught us about their technology, we could help with the repairs and complete them faster.

The Urai male looked at Fen. They touched one another's heads for a few moments before turning back towards the engineer.

He touched his speech pad and answered, "We believe that you will be able to assist. We will attempt to teach you about our technology. Perhaps that will allow us to complete our repairs more rapidly."

Rouhr, who had been talking with Vidia and the team leaders, looked over at Fen. "Thank you, Fen. You have been more of a savior than any of us could have expected."

While the conversations about repairs and defenses continued, I looked over to Amira, who stood by a window, her gaze fixed on something outside.

I wondered what point of the conversation had caught in her bright, agile mind.

Knowing her, it could be anything.

Somehow, that made me nervous.

And terribly, terribly interested.

AMIRA

My mind raced after the meeting. I couldn't get past what Fen had said. I had to know more.

I chased her through the massive corridors of the *Aurora*. When I finally caught up to her, she didn't seem surprised to see me, though it was hard to tell for sure.

Without a mouth, her face wasn't as expressive as mine or the other alien species. Her eyes didn't reflect emotion the same way, either.

If I had to guess, she was amused.

She laid a delicate hand on her speech pad. "You have questions."

I nodded.

She made a sweeping gesture with her arm, inviting me to walk beside her.

"I want to know more about what you think the Xathi are up to," I said.

"Of course. As I said before, I believe they are experimenting with different methods of psychological indoctrination. Why they would do this? I do not know. Perhaps they wish to build up their armies, so they themselves do not have to fight. Perhaps they are trying to integrate more species into theirs."

"But you also said that the Xathi could be looking for something."

"It is possible. However, it is less likely than my first theory."

"I wonder what made the Xathi decide to start indoctrinating humans," I wondered out loud.

Fen gave me what I assume was a curious look. "What do you mean?"

"When the Xathi first landed, they quickly ransacked the capital city. They decimated some smaller towns. They would've taken over Duvest completely if the *Vengeance* crew hadn't stepped in," I explained. "It appeared that they were hell-bent on taking over the planet, then they suddenly changed tactics. It's just strange, I guess."

Not that everything else that was happening wasn't strange.

"I did not know that," Fen said slowly. "And they haven't raided other cities since?"

"Not in the same way. Our human doctor just traveled to Einhiv, where there were no Xathi, but the place had been completely infested with hybrids. Einhiv was almost completely overrun, and the Xathi didn't lift a finger, other than somehow creating the hybrids."

"That changes things," Fen said thoughtfully.

"So, you think the Xathi are after something specific?"

"Now I believe so. It is possible a single Xathi stumbled upon a human, or a small group of humans, that possessed knowledge of something the Xathi found useful. When the queen learned of it, she sent her soldiers to hunt it down, made hybrids to try to infect others with more information. Follow me."

Fen lead me deep into the *Aurora*. After several minutes of walking through confusing and nearly identical halls, we stopped at an unmarked door.

It slid open to reveal a sophisticated control room, the walls made up entirely of screens. Some reflected the surveillance footage from the micro-cameras mounted around the ship, others reflected ever-changing charts and maps of the surrounding area.

"There are a handful of races that have produced technology that the Xathi have shown great interest in," Fen explained. "Humans are not one of those races. No offense."

"None taken."

"Is there anything on this planet that makes the humans who live here different from the humans on your original planet?"

"We're more ecologically minded," I answered. "Much of what we use can be recycled into something else. The first colonies on this planet had to be completely self-sufficient until more resources could be found. Wasting and exploiting resources is what cost us Earth in the first place, so we've always been careful of that here."

"The Xathi are already masters at collecting and refining resources," Fen pondered.

"Even if those resources are living beings." The words were sour on my tongue.

"Yes." Fen allowed herself to become lost in thought for a moment.

I'd heard that her people, as well as others, had been on this ship when the Xathi queen did something to their minds. Whatever the queen did caused the beings on this ship to open the airlock and cast themselves out into the void of space.

The only reason Fen survived was because she and a handful of other Urai had been in stasis pods. I couldn't imagine waking up in the middle of a forest only to find out that my ship had crashed and nearly everyone on board was dead.

"Is there a chance any other races inhabited this planet before the humans did?" Fen snapped herself out of her silence.

"When planets were first being scouted for sustainability, it was widely believed this one was never before inhabited. However, no one was checking very thoroughly. Getting off Earth was a time-sensitive operation. Those in charge of finding new homes were looking for something that was safe and something we could get to with our available ships."

"What do you believe?" Fen's question caught me by surprise.

I don't think anyone, outside of school, had really asked me that before.

"There is a small group of people who believe that something did live here before us, but not in the area that we've settled." I ran my hand through my hair, half-embarrassed. "I'm one of them, I guess."

"Why hasn't this theory been investigated?" she asked.

"It hasn't been a priority. The evidence is nothing more than a few blurry images from a satellite, some wonky readings. I've seen them myself, they truly aren't much to go on."

"Then why do you believe?"

It was a question I'd gotten a lot, particularly from my parents when I decided to go to school for archaeology. They couldn't understand why I would put so much effort into a career that wasn't of use to the colonies.

As a child, I'd hoarded data pads filled with stories of the oldest societies on Earth. It's been a lifelong fascination. I couldn't imagine doing anything else.

"Up until very recently, humans believed we were the only ones," I explained. "It wasn't until the Xathi and the *Vengeance* fell through the rift that we knew for certain there were other intelligent species. But I never believed we were the only ones. The universe is too big and too mysterious for me to completely eliminate that possibility."

"It is wise of you to look beyond what you think is known." Fen nodded in approval.

"If you exist, if the Xathi exist, if beings like Dax and Vrehx exist, then why couldn't others have existed? And lived here, for that matter?"

"Let's find out then, shall we?" Fen asked with a sly gleam in her glittering eyes.

"What do you mean?" I couldn't help but feel excited.

"The *Aurora* is equipped with satellites that make human satellites look like children's toys. Again, no offense," she added, her tone sheepish. Maybe.

"Again, none taken," I laughed.

"Where do people believe an ancient society would

have lived?" Fen touched the screen displaying a map of the wetlands and zoomed out until it showed the entire planet.

"The least investigated area on this planet is a desert region almost on the other side of the world." I stepped closer to Fen and reached out to position the map in the correct place. "If I had to guess, this would be the place."

Fen moved to another screen to calibrate a satellite. "It'll draw a bit of power to send up a stealth satellite, but since we're using the rift as a reserve, I doubt it will affect much." She took her hand away from her speech pad to use the complex control panel.

"A stealth satellite? I thought we were protected behind those sonic barriers?"

"Just because we are safe doesn't mean we should draw attention to ourselves. Besides, we don't want the Xathi to realize we are looking for something. They'll start looking, too."

"That's a good point. How long will it take for us to see the results? A few hours?"

Impatience coursed through me. If there was evidence of some long-gone society on this planet, I wanted to know. Now.

I'd been dreaming about something like this since I was a little kid.

"More like a minute," Fen replied. On the wall to our

left, one of the screens shifted to show a grid map that was becoming more detailed by the second. "It looks like the satellite has located a likely area. It's re-oriented itself and is refining the results now."

"I can't believe this!" I was practically squealing and jumping up and down. Probably I should have tried to be more professional, less impulsive about this, but hell, who was I kidding.

No matter how hard I tried, I was still me. And this was worth making some noise about.

The grid map showed a cluster of simple lines. After zooming in, the lines resembled some sort of multi-level structure beneath the surface. Parts of it were incomplete and fragmented, suggesting that areas had collapsed over time.

When I was in school, classes were taught on the ancient cultures and ruins of Earth. The ruins appearing on the grid map didn't resemble any of these, which wasn't a surprise. But if I had to make a comparison, the geometric shape of the structures was like the old Mayan temples, except they were made with the intention of being underground.

"There's something there!" I exclaimed. "There's really something out there! I knew it! We have to go find out what it is!"

"There is an Urai aboard this ship who has long

studied the races the Xathi target. I am sure he will be eager to accompany you on your journey," Fen offered.

Her race was old enough, perhaps *she* was old enough, to have witnessed the rise, fall, and rediscovery of many civilizations. I must've looked a bit insane to her, but I couldn't care less.

"That would be amazing," I gushed. I'd never gushed before in my life, but I couldn't help it.

A fire had ignited in my chest that I hadn't felt since I was a little girl playing explorer alone in my room. It was more than just having the chance to discover something no one had ever found before.

If these ruins were built by one of the races the Xathi were interested in, and if there was something inside them that the Xathi wanted, I could get to it first. It could change the tide of the war.

But I couldn't do this alone.

I needed help and I knew just who to ask.

DAXION

After the general meeting, while Rouhr was still planning with the team leaders, I had been asked to help Evie and Vidia with getting everyone settled.

Anyone who needed medical attention was sent to the med bay for Evie and Nyx, the Urai medical specialist, to check out.

Many of the humans were wary or scared of Nyx and crowded the portion of the med bay that Evie was in.

It sort of made sense.

The Urai were an unusual looking race, but no more unusual than a walking killer tree or crystalline insects.

For the people who weren't injured, Vidia and I helped them to find quarters and to stop any bickering that happened when a person or family didn't get a room they wanted. It surprised me to see humans fighting over a room, especially since they were virtually identical and a gift from a race of people who had graciously given over quarters that had once belonged to their own friends, family, and crew.

When I mentioned that, most of the complaining humans stopped talking and accepted their assignments.

After getting everyone situated with rooms and into the med bay, I was tasked with finding everyone who had some sort of skill that could benefit the ship—things like electrical knowledge, carpentry, engineering, anything of the sort—and to send them to General Rouhr for assignments.

If anyone grumbled, I asked them if they would like to help get rid of the Xathi or if they would like to go out into the wilderness alone, without weapons or tools, and deal with them on their own. It quieted everyone that complained. I loved the looks on their faces when I gave them the proposal. It was genuinely entertaining.

As I finished directing people to the general, I decided to find my team to see if there was anything I could help with. As I rounded one of the corners, I nearly bumped into Amira.

"Oh, I've been looking for you," she said as we

stepped back from one another. She looked a bit agitated or excited. "I need some advice."

Despite my surprise, a warmth spread through my gut.

"Since when do you ask anyone for advice?"

"I know I haven't been the friendliest person around, and you deserve better treatment from not just me, but from all of us." She pursed her lips, regret clear on her face. "You and your people have risked your lives to keep us safe, and I appreciate it. I came to you because you're one of the most level-headed people I know, and I wanted your opinion and advice on an idea I had."

I was flattered, and... something else. Something I didn't want to spend too much time thinking about.

"Thank you." I figured I would get straight to the point. "What was your idea?"

She could barely contain her excitement as she told me.

"Well, Fen launched a satellite into orbit, and we used it to get a scan of the planet, something we haven't been able to do ourselves, at least not on this kind of level. The Urai technology is so far more advanced than ours." She wrung her hands together as she spoke, eyes wide with excitement. "Anyway, what I was saying was that we ran a scan of the planet and found something."

"What did you find?" My own curiosity was now piqued.

She nearly bounced as the smile on her face spread from ear to ear. "We found ruins! Ruins we never knew existed before, or at least I never knew about. I don't exactly have access to government information or computers. Maybe that's why the Xathi stopped attacking," she said with a tilt of her head. "Maybe they found someone who did have access, who already knew, or suspected."

She shook her head, looked back up at me, and continued, "The ruins might hold the answers we need. They're older than anything else I've ever seen on this planet and they're in—or is it on?—oh well, they're on a massive land mass about a day's travel from here. Fen says it's worth looking into and I agree."

I held up my hands to slow her down. "Wait. Let me make sure I understand this correctly. You and Fen found some ruins about a day's flight from here, and you want to go check it out to see if it holds any information or anything that could potentially be used against the Xathi? Yes?" I had to take a breath.

"Yes! Yes. Exactly!"

I thought about it for a few moments. It certainly couldn't hurt too much to investigate. Amira and Fen might be correct in thinking that the ruins could hold something we needed. At worst, it would simply be a waste of two or three days and a little bit of fuel.

"Okay. I like the idea."

"You do? Oh, thank you. Thank you, thank you, thank you, thank you, thank you!" She nearly squealed as she jumped forward and gave me a quick hug.

"Hold on," I said sternly, trying to calm her down, hating to be the one to wipe even a trace of excitement from her smile. "We still need to speak to General Rouhr and ask his permission. If he approves, we go. If he doesn't, we let it go for now."

"But we *need* to go there, and we need to be first. What if the Xathi go after it and find whatever is there before we do?"

"Then we convince the general to let us go. Come." I motioned for her to walk with me.

We made our way to the general and had to wait a few minutes as he finished discussing plans and handing out assignments to the people I had sent him. When he was finished, he saw Amira and me and motioned for us to approach.

"What can I do for you, Dax?" He sat back in his chair.

The general looked exhausted. While he was doing a fantastic job of hiding it, I was sure the stress of everything that had happened was wearing him down.

I couldn't blame him.

We had lost, badly, and it had cost us our home, and most of our supplies.

We were relying on the Urai, but they had no weapons, so all we had was what we managed to bring along in our escape. There would be a mission soon to try and retrieve as many supplies and munitions as we could from the *Vengeance*. Something had to be left.

There just had to be.

Amira brought me out of my thoughts when she cleared her throat to speak. "General, sir. First, thank you for rescuing us and doing everything you can to try to fight off the Xathi. If no one has said it yet, I want to be the first to say thank you, and that we appreciate what you and your people have done."

He motioned to a chair for her to sit. I remained standing behind her.

Amira looked up at me, then looked back at Rouhr. With a deep breath, she laid out her idea.

She told the general about finding the ruins and how Fen believed there might be something there that could be of interest to us. She wanted to organize a small search party to go check it out.

Rouhr shook his head. "I'm sorry. But I can't sanction such an action, not after everything that has just happened. You must understand, we've just lost everything…our supplies, our weapons, our munitions, and whatever advantage we might have had over the

Xathi. We aren't even on the mainland anymore, and that takes us away from the friends we've made there."

"I understand that, sir. But, if Fen is correct in her evaluation of the scan, these ruins are sensationally old and could belong to a race that the Xathi are interested in. If they're interested in it, we need to be interested in it. What if there is something there that could help us? Or, if not help us, at least finding it keeps it out of Xathi hands...claws...whatever, and that still helps us."

Her argument was compelling. If, and that was a big if, there was something in the ruins that the Xathi wanted, it made sense to make sure they couldn't get to it.

"How do you know they want it?" Rouhr asked.

Amira shook her head. "I don't, sir. But," she leaned forward, her hands held in front of her, "what if they are? Fen told me that the Xathi are obsessed with finding advanced technology from certain races. What if one of the humans had information about the ruins, and that's what changed the Xathi behavior? What if, and I'm only the third generation here, mind you... what if someone already found something and tried to keep it a secret, and it was found out by someone before the Xathi arrived? Sir, this could be important to all of us."

Her passionate tone had me convinced, and I could see that the general was weighing her words.

I decided to tip the scales. "Sir, what if she's right? What if this really is something the Xathi want to investigate? Wouldn't it make sense to be the first ones there? The worst that could happen is Amira and I spend three days wasting fuel."

He looked up at me, a determined look on his face. "It wouldn't be just you and Amira. I want you to take a small team...*very* small team...with you. No more than four or five people in total."

"You're letting us go?" Amira asked.

With a nod, Rouhr said, "Yes, I am. It makes sense. Right now, we've lost advantages. If we can find one, no matter how slim the odds, then we need to take the chance. Go, and be careful."

Amira and I nodded. She said "thank you" about a dozen times, and we headed out.

Amira beamed happiness, and I couldn't help but smile at her. She was overjoyed at the prospect, and I was happy as well. The general was right, we needed something, anything, to give us a chance and this just might be that thing.

Rouhr was taking a gamble that we would find something.

If he was right, the advantage would be ours.

If not...then the end would be that much nearer.

AMIRA

Dax was the easy part. There was one other person I wanted to ask for help, but I wasn't sure how to do it.

Mariella was an archivist. She was an expert at finding the paper trail, so to speak, left behind by people of the past.

It was her skills that had led her to discover the source of an illness that plagued her family. Her help would be invaluable if we found documents or datapads in the ruins. Even if we couldn't read the text, she had the uncanny ability to figure the next logical step, often a way to crack it all open.

Mariella had been friendly to me at first. She made several attempts to invite me to eat with her and her sister, Leena, at mealtimes.

But I never accepted her offers, and eventually, she stopped asking.

On the other hand, her sister was a hard-ass who wasn't interested in playing nice.

Well, she used to be. She relaxed a hell of a lot after she started seeing Axtin. Once, she even said hello to me in the refugee bay.

It was weird.

I guess happiness did that to people. Maybe after I talked to Mariella, I could ask Leena for some tips.

Making friendships and forming social bonds didn't come naturally to me. After our parents died and Jeneva left, I started pushing people away. I didn't want to be left again.

It was a pretty great system up until now. Now I had to depend more on the goodwill of others than I'd ever had to before.

And some people, I didn't mind getting to know better. A green-striped face flashed in my mind, and I pushed it away.

No time to be thinking of that.

Not now. Probably not ever.

And now I needed to focus on something else, quick.

"Hey, Mariella." My hand jerked in a pathetic motion that somewhat resembled a wave.

She was surprised to see me. It was written all over her face.

"Hi, Amira!" she said brightly. "What's up?"

"Actually, I need a favor."

Nerves twisted in my stomach. She was going to say no. I'd turned away when she tried to be friendly before. I'd been prickly, my normal bitchy self. Now she hated me, and she'd never agree to a potentially dangerous mission.

Never.

"Sure! What do you need?"

That caught me off guard. I hadn't even given her any details yet, and she was already agreeing to help me. I needed to take a page out of her book.

"It's actually a pretty big favor," I clarified. "And you absolutely don't have to go, but…," I pulled up the scans from Fen's satellite on a datapad. "Fen and I found ruins. General Rouhr has given me permission to put together a small team to investigate. I thought you'd be perfect for it."

Mariella's face lit up like the *Aurora's* control room. "Yes! That sounds amazing! When do we leave? I can be ready in an hour!"

I couldn't help but laugh. This must've been how I looked to Fen when the satellite image came in.

The pressure lifted off my chest. Now that I'd asked,

I felt ridiculous for being so nervous. I wondered if I'd ever stop expecting the worst of people.

"Dax is picking out the best transport unit to get us there. Apparently, the Urai have some good options. He can give you all the details," I explained.

"Okay!" Mariella leaped to her feet immediately. "This is going to be such an adventure. I'm so excited!"

She had a slight skip in her step as she hurried away.

I felt the same way, honestly.

"I'll go too!" A voice from behind startled me. I whirled around to find Ren standing uncomfortably close.

"You scared the hell out of me. Wear a bell or something." I put a hand over my chest, as if that would still my fluttering heart.

"Sorry." He chuckled. "But if you and Mariella are going somewhere, I should come, too."

"Why?"

He seemed hurt that I didn't match his enthusiasm. "If you're going out with a bunch of aliens, I should be there."

"A small team was approved for this. I can't just bring random people."

Something wasn't right.

I couldn't place it, but my gut was screaming at me to keep Ren as far away from this mission as possible.

"Who else is going?" His eyes gleamed. "And why? We just got here."

"We're just familiarizing some of the crew with the area," I lied quickly. "It's nothing serious or scary, so you can relax."

I wasn't sure if he believed me or not. I walked away before he could say anything.

All the stress of the last few months must have gotten to him. I made a note to ask Dr. Parr to look at him after we got back.

I went to gather supplies for the trip, but quickly realized I didn't have any supplies. The few things I owned were still on the *Vengeance,* and none of it was suitable for fieldwork.

Lucky for me, I wasn't far from any of the main common areas. I'd had a hard enough time getting my bearings on the *Vengeance.* The *Aurora* was going to be a completely new beast to tame.

Vidia had set up a system for finding people new rooms. One of the Urai who worked alongside her was kind enough to take me to the room Vidia had found for me.

I felt strange being in there. Not long ago, it had belonged to someone who'd gone mad and willingly flushed themselves out of an airlock. There were two beds in the cabin. I wondered who my roommate would be.

The Urai mentioned there was clothing for me, as well. I opened the small closet. Thankfully, whoever these clothes belonged to before me had also had two arms and two legs in the same configuration as I did.

Or was their technology so advanced they'd been able to start manufacturing human clothing already?

I found a pair of sturdy boots that were slightly too big, but I remedied that with a wad of fabric in the heel. I also found pants with plenty of pockets that fit almost perfectly.

All the tops were too big around my shoulders, but I found a small bit of something like elastic to fix that. It was as good as it was going to get, and I had more important things to do than worry about my fashion style.

I was the last one to make it to the *Aurora's* docking bay. Dax had picked out a sleek little shuttle that had just enough room for us all. Fen was there as well, standing with another Urai, a male.

"This is Zan." I shook the Urai's hand, though the gesture appeared to confuse him. "He's our resident tech master, and he knows quite a bit about the races the Xathi are interested in."

"I'm looking forward to assisting you on this mission," Zan spoke in a professional manner. "Though, in my expert opinion, the likelihood that these ruins belong to one of those races is highly unlikely."

"It's still worth looking into," I replied.

Zan gave a sharp nod before climbing into the transport unit.

"What a ray of sunshine," Dax murmured.

I held back a snort.

"I hope you don't mind if Tu'ver comes along," Mariella bounded over to me. "He'd feel better if he was there to keep an eye on me. I think it's a good idea. Sometimes I don't always think things through."

"At least you admit it," Tu'ver said with a quiet smirk. "She wanted to walk into a toxic cavern once."

"It's true," Mariella admitted.

"Didn't she cause a rockslide that brought down half a mountain?" Dax wondered.

"Technically, Tu'ver started the rockslide," Mariella said in defense.

"It was your idea," Tu'ver corrected.

"Are you sure you want these two to come along?" Dax asked me in jest.

"At the very least, it'll be entertaining," I laughed.

"And you need someone to pilot this thing." Tu'ver slapped his hand against the hull.

"Wouldn't Zan be the pilot?" I asked. He was a Urai, after all, and this was a Urai transport unit.

"Apparently," Dax whispered so Zan wouldn't hear, "he knows how it all works, but he's afraid of heights."

"The poor thing," Mariella hummed with sympathy.

"He'll be okay," Dax assured her. "From where he's sitting, it's almost impossible to tell we're flying, aside from the movement."

That made Mariella feel better. She allowed Tu'ver to help her into the transport unit. Tu'ver went around to the pilot's station to make sure everything was in working order.

"So, what's the plan once we get there?" Dax asked.

"According to the scans, the ruins are underground. So, the first thing we're going to do is figure out how to get inside," I explained.

"And then?"

"No clue."

Dax tipped his head back and laughed. "Glad to know you've thought this through."

Tu'ver signaled that he was ready to head out. I climbed into the transport unit and Dax slid in beside me. The transport unit moved so smoothly, the only way I knew we'd taken off was by looking out the window.

"Excited?" Dax asked.

"You have no idea."

This was going to be fun.

DAXION

Tu'ver piloted us along in one of the *Aurora's* small, personal shuttles. Zan, our new Urai friend, had helped Tu'ver learn the incredibly simple controls. Even Axtin could have flown this, and he was stunningly inept when it came to piloting things.

As fast as the craft was, it would still take us nearly a day to make it to the ruins. Mariella had brought out a tablet and taught Amira and me a game she called chess. It was an interesting game, full of strategy. Amira took to it quickly, beating me several times before I finally understood the rules and figured out how to plan my moves.

I showed the women a game we used to play back home that also involved strategy and planning. They weren't fans, as it involved some very brutal tactics and the simulation was, as they said, gross.

We talked a bit, discussing Mariella's work and Amira's passion for archaeology. I shared stories of my siblings, my pride in them apparent as I smiled when I spoke of them.

Amira said it was nice that I took care of my family so much, it was something that some of her own kind didn't do. Even on a small world such as this, there were still so many humans that were selfish and thought only of what benefitted them. I told her that the Valorni were the same, until the Xathi attacked.

Zan wasn't much of a contributor to the conversations. He was interested in the tablet Mariella used, as well as the games we had played, but seemed to stay away from our conversations. The little bit that he did contribute to our conversations at least let me know that he was a decent enough character for me to trust, to a point.

Eventually Mariella went up front to spend some time with Tu'ver. Zan concentrated on his equipment, essentially ignoring the rest of us. That left Amira and me to talk and play games.

After a few more rounds, I looked up front to see Tu'ver showing Mariella the controls and stifling a yawn.

None of us had had a chance to really rest or recover from the attack.

My own eyes seemed a bit heavy, as well.

"You look tired," Amira whispered.

I stifled my yawn as I nodded. "Just a bit. I'll be fine though," I tried to reassure her. Too many people had left her alone, let her push them away.

I wasn't going to be one of them.

She shook her head at me. "No, get some sleep. We're still a long way off and you need your rest. I'll keep Mariella company." She stood up and moved to the front as Tu'ver came towards the back.

He nodded at me and sat down, getting himself comfortable. Within seconds, he was asleep, something I always admired about him. He once told me that he had trained himself to fall asleep quickly, but I was never able to figure out how.

I fidgeted a bit to get myself comfortable and stared at the ceiling, thinking of the mission ahead.

Could there really be something of value there?

Would the Xathi be on our trail, or could we finally have a clear win?

And if there was nothing, if the trip was a waste of time, how much would it hurt Amira?

When I woke up several hours later, Tu'ver was back at the front and Amira was snuggled against me, sound asleep. It felt comfortable to have her leaning against my shoulder.

Not just comfortable, right.

Mariella smiled at me and gave me a wink as she brought Tu'ver a drink.

"How much longer?" I asked quietly.

Tu'ver looked back and smiled. "Not long, my giant friend. Less than an hour."

I nodded and sat back, my eyes closed as I tried to clear my mind, but the soft body pressed into mine distracted me, made my usual pre-battle routines more difficult than ever.

When we came within view of land, there was nothing. It was barren desert and sand dunes everywhere. The only vegetation on the ground looked sick or dying. I could almost see the heat radiating off the ground.

"We're nearly there, better get ready," Tu'ver announced.

I watched Amira, still asleep on my shoulder. She looked so peaceful, a strand of hair just slightly covering her cheek, a tiny little snore finding its way from her mouth. I didn't want to wake her, but it was time.

"Amira. Hey," I said quietly as I lifted her upright.

Her sleepy, unfocused gaze met mine, then her eyes opened wide, breath quickening.

Heat raced through me like a bolt across my gut as I brushed the wayward strand of hair away.

The soft skin of her cheek tempted me to stroke it, to explore, but this wasn't the time.

"We're here," I forced out.

She blinked, soft eyes slowly focusing on the day before us, on our mission. But for just a second, she rested her cheek in my palm.

"Thanks for being my pillow."

Then she left in a blaze of activity, bouncing between Mariella and Zan, and the moment was gone.

I forced Amira's touch to the back of my mind. The heat was nearly unbearable when compared to the comfortable environment of the ship.

We stepped out, the sun behind us, and took stock of our surroundings. It wasn't much to take in...sand, dirt, brownness, more brownness, and the only green was a pair of bushes turning brown.

"Well, this is dismal," Tu'ver commented. "Are you sure your ruins are here?"

Amira looked around. "Yes, going by Fen's satellite readings. It makes sense if you think about it. These ruins may be thousands of years old. When the land was inhabited, it probably looked much different. And then they left, or died out, and nature took over."

"Not much to look at if this is nature," Tu'ver snorted.

I had to agree with him.

Amira chewed her bottom lip. "It has to be here. Even the early scans of the planet before our grandparents landed here showed that this land mass was livable. Humans *could* survive here. Surely another civilization could have, as well."

Tu'ver shook his head and walked a little bit away to check out our surroundings. I looked over at Zan, to see him looking distressed. "What is it, Zan?" I asked.

He looked up at me, a flash of surprise on his face, then it was gone. He put his hand to his speech pad and answered. "The environment is disrupting my equipment. Nothing seems to be working properly. It is quite disconcerting."

"Maybe we're in the wrong place?" Mariella suggested.

Zan shook his head emphatically, something I never noticed Fen do. "No," he said, his tone very defensive. "Our equipment is beyond reproach. If our satellite pinpointed these coordinates, then these coordinates are where we should be. I assisted with the design of that satellite myself. I can assure you that it is in proper working order."

"Sorry," Mariella said.

Zan brought his hand up to his speech pad again, but I interrupted them both.

"Easy. Everyone take it easy. I trust your satellite,

Zan, but I agree with Mariella. We might be in the wrong place."

Zan gave me a look that spoke volumes. How could I believe in his tech yet still think Mariella was right? "What if Amira's statement about nature taking over is correct? This is a desert, and from what I know of deserts, sand is constantly blown around and sometimes covers things. What if the entryway to the complex is below us?"

Zan nodded, then responded, "That is a logical explanation. However, due to the environmental interference with my equipment, I cannot determine nor hypothesize how far below our feet the ruins may be. It could be only a few feet."

"Or it could be a few hundred feet," Tu'ver finished. "This may have been a waste of time. We don't have the equipment needed for an excavation."

As Tu'ver, Zan, Mariella, and I debated on what should happen next, I watched Amira pace back and forth. I could tell she was agitated, and angry, and I couldn't blame her. This had been her idea, I had encouraged her, and the idea that we had made it here to find nothing was frustrating.

Eventually, the four of us agreed that our best course of action was to return to the *Aurora* and report back to Rouhr and Fen.

"No!" Amira said forcefully when we told her. "No. I

will not give up this quickly. Like you said, it could be just right under our feet. I will not leave until I know what's here."

The others looked at me and I sighed.

I walked up to Amira, who had sat down on a flat rock, the only flat rock in a sea of jagged, craggy rocks. "Amira, please understand. We are, all of us, in a foreign land with no knowledge of where these ruins are. The equipment we had counted on to assist us is malfunctioning." I tried to reason with her, but she steadfastly refused to look at me, as if focused on something else.

She scratched at the rock she sat on, shaking her head as I spoke.

I looked at the others, lost. I didn't know what else to do. I turned back to her and opened my mouth to talk. My mouth stayed open as a small hatch in the rock popped open next to her, a button inside.

"Hm—mmm," she smiled at me smugly as she indicated the small hatch. "I told you something was here. You don't just put a flat rock in the middle of a bunch of craggy ones and not go investigate it." Then she pressed the button. The ground around us began to shake. As the others retreated a few steps, I grabbed Amira and we ran back towards the others.

The sand shifted and fell, revealing a ramp leading down.

After a minute or so, the sand stopped.

We inched our way to the edge of the ramp and looked down, far down. At the bottom of the ramp was a perfectly square opening, leading further down into the ground.

"Finally," Zan said, straightening. "My readings are beginning to resolve." He stood at the edge of the opening, then strode down the ramp, eyes fixed on an instrument panel.

"Are you certain this is safe?" Tu'ver asked, arm wrapped around Mariella's shoulders. From the press of her lips, I could guess his grip was all that kept her from running after the Urai.

"Of course," came the snapped reply. "I'm an expert at this."

Tu'ver cocked an eyebrow in my direction, and I shrugged. That's why the guy was here, right?

Tu'ver and Mariella followed.

I glanced down at Amira. "I expected you to be racing Zan to the door."

Her eyes shone with excitement. "I just can't believe it's real," she whispered, her small hand creeping into mine. "It's really real."

I laced my fingers with hers, squeezing gently.

"Come on, let's see what else is down there."

Mariella and Tu'ver had caught up with Zan by the

time we started our descent. As we continued down, the shadows grew longer, until the desert heat chilled.

"What did they build with that could have lasted in perfect condition for so long?" Amira wondered as she gazed around us. "The mechanism didn't rust. Well, there's not enough water for that now, I suppose. But the sand didn't clog it, everything seems to be working perfectly."

I touched the smooth surface. "Some sort of plex, maybe, fashioned to look like stone?" I shook my head. "I haven't seen anything like it."

"Surely this wasn't meant for foot traffic," she continued. "The ramp is smooth enough, but that opening looks wide enough for some sort of vehicle."

A niggling worry grew in the back of my head.

"I wonder, if it's not supposed to be approached this way, if Zan's devices can check for--"

A sharp click echoed from the walls, and the floor dropped from beneath our feet.

AMIRA

"Hang on to something!" Dax shouted as the desert expanse disappeared and we tumbled down into darkness.

"Like what?" I shrieked. I clawed at the smooth surface of the trap chute. We weren't falling straight down. The smooth surface was more like a ramp or a slide. We slid so fast I couldn't be certain, but it felt like one solid piece of glassy rock.

"I don't know! Just try to slow yourself down!" Dax shouted. That turned out to be much easier than it sounded. The slide suddenly stopped. We were dumped unceremoniously onto a flat floor. My tailbone barked in protest as I landed ass first.

"Dax?" I called into the darkness. I heard a grunt in response. "Oh, good. You made it down." Another grunt. "Do you still have the flashlight or any of your gear?" I asked.

"I think the flashlight would be the thing jabbing into my ribs," Dax groaned. I heard him fumbling for a minute, then a beam of light burst forth to my left.

"Can you stand?" I asked. My body ached from head to toe, but I didn't think anything was broken.

"Yeah," Dax grunted. The beam danced and jiggled as Dax stood. He shone the light along the pitch-black floor until he found me. I lifted a hand to shield myself from the assault of blinding light.

"Give me your hand." I reached up and allowed Dax to pull me onto my feet. Some of my bones popped and groaned.

"That doesn't sound good," Dax said, alarmed.

"It's fine. Human bones do that sometimes. Especially after they fall a few hundred feet." I rubbed the small of my back. "Where do you think we are?"

Dax shone the light around the room. It was of fair size and looked perfectly square. The surface of the walls, floor, and high ceiling was all the same seamless black stone, so polished, I could see my own reflection in the wavering light.

It was an architectural marvel, but there was one troubling detail.

There wasn't a door.

"How are we supposed to get out?" I asked in a

small voice. I'd read about Old Earth structures like this riddled with traps like this. The idea was to prevent thieves from escaping. Sometimes, the thieves would make it out alive but that was only if the guards checked the trap pits. Otherwise, the thieves just died.

There were no guards here.

Or if there were, I wasn't sure I wanted to meet them.

"We'll figure something out." Dax sounded so confident.

I wondered if it was genuine.

I felt the opposite of confident. I felt panicked and guilty.

"If we don't get out of here, it's my fault for getting you into this mess in the first place." My chest constricted. "I never should've pushed this mission. I didn't think it through. I always screw things up." I wouldn't cry in front of Dax

"That's nonsense, and you know it." Dax was by my side in an instant. He laid his large hand on my back with surprising gentleness. "General Rouhr wouldn't have approved anything if he didn't think it was important. You found the opening. Zan was the one who plunged ahead without checking."

"But-"

"No buts," he said sternly. "This isn't your fault. You

didn't mess anything up." He rubbed my back in small, soothing circles.

After a few moments, I nodded. He was right. Whatever had happened, we were here. Falling apart wouldn't help anything.

"Okay," I sucked in a breath. "What are we looking for?"

"Anything that stands out." Dax swung the flashlight around the room. Nothing immediately jumped out so we opted for a more thorough approach. Dax took one side of the room, I took the other. I ran my hand along the smooth surface of the wall, feeling for any irregularities while Dax searched with the light.

I wasn't sure how much time had passed. It could've been hours. I paced along a stretch of wall for what felt like the hundredth time when my fingers trailed over the slightest divot in the wall.

"Dax!" I exclaimed. "Bring the light over here. I think I've got something." Light flooded the area. Sure enough, there was a hair-thin line running vertically from the floor and stopping about six feet up before going right at a perfect angle. The horizontal divot continued for a few more feet before turning back down to the floor.

"That looks like it could be a doorway," Dax said thoughtfully. He pounded on it as hard as he could with his fist and then pounded on another part of the wall a few feet over. "This part of the wall isn't as dense."

I pounded my fist in the same places he did. All that did was hurt my hand.

"They feel the same to me." I shook my wrist and rubbed the side of my hand.

Dax laughed softly.

"Just trust me on this," he said. "And hold this." He tossed the flashlight in my direction and stepped back until he was almost against the opposite wall. He drew his crossbow and readied a bolt.

"I'd move if I were you," he suggested.

"What are you doing?" I asked, moving as far away from the potential door as possible.

"This." Dax loosed the bolt. I expected it to bounce off the stone, but it stuck fast in the dead center of the secret door. I stared, open-mouthed, between Dax and his bolt.

"How is that possible?" I marveled.

"That's not even the most entertaining part." Dax motioned for me to stand by him. I obliged. "Watch."

At first, nothing happened. I was about to ask Dax why he asked me to stare at a wall when I noticed faint tendrils of smoke coming from the tip of the bolt.

"What the hell?" I wondered out loud.

"I coat my bolts in a toxic, corrosive acid. It can eat

through anything, except the bolt material," Dax explained.

"Anything?"

"Well, everything I've tried it on so far," Dax amended. "You sister actually helped me find ingredients to make more when I ran out here." I walked closer to the bolt and peered as close as I dared. Sure enough, the stone nearest to the barbed head of the bolt was bubbling and hissing. Small chunks of rock crumbled away.

"You did it," I said, quietly, watching him. Kind, handsome, and smart, in a possibly disturbingly destructive way.

"Don't thank me yet. It'll take a while for the toxin to eat through the stone."

That didn't matter, he'd still saved us. We could still survey the ruins.

Excitement bubbled up inside me so quickly that, before I knew what I was doing, I ran back to Dax and threw my arms around his neck.

For once, I'd caught him off guard.

He pretended to stagger back, laughing before enclosing his arms around me.

"How many more times are you going to save my ass?" I looked up at him, then froze as our eyes met, sparks pooling in my belly.

"As many times as I need to." The words sounded

like a joke, but his intense expression meant something else.

Something solid.

Trustable.

I'd never really had a boyfriend. Sure, there were harmless crushes and flirtations when I was younger, but never anything serious.

Mainly, it was because I had never looked up to a male figure.

Never respected one.

Never been awed by one.

Until Daxion.

His strength was intense. His brute force that he wielded with the precision of a surgeon was enough to make me daydream.

His caring nature was enough to give my heart flutters.

And his touch stirred something in me, a heat I didn't think I'd ever feel.

And in this pit, in an alien ruin, with a war on the other side of the world and our friends possibly in danger, one mad thought drowned out everything else.

I wanted him to kiss me.

As if reading my mind Dax dipped his head and brought his mouth to mine.

Electricity shot through my body at the touch of his

lips. I tightened my grip, pulling myself closer to him as he deepened the kiss.

One of his hands reached up to grasp the back of my neck, holding me to him. My heart pounded in my chest. I wondered if Dax could feel it too.

Dax effortlessly lifted me off the ground. I wrapped my legs around his waist, tugging him closer as he moved, until my back was pressed against the cool surface of the black stone walls. I arched against the wall, pressing my chest into his as I kissed up his neck until I found his mouth once more.

I felt the evidence of his arousal pressing against my inner thigh and my heart skipped a beat. With a shuddering breath, I realized how much I wanted him.

The world fell away. The room, the trap door, even the ruins themselves ceased to exist to me.

Right here, right now, all I saw was him.

Feeling bold, I slid my hands under his shirt. I explored the ridges of solid muscle around to his back and up his broad shoulders. I nearly jumped out of my skin when he did the same. One hand wandered to my back, the other snaked up to grab my breast. He nipped at my neck, chuckled when goosebumps appeared on my skin.

If he asked, I would let him take me.

I wanted him to take me.

The sound of rock shattering broke the spell. We

broke apart. I felt lightheaded and completely exhilarated as I slid down the wall onto my feet. Dax breathed heavily, looking like he was coming out of a daze.

I was the first to look away, forcing my focus to the wall. Still impassible, but a sizable chunk had crumbled to the floor.

Right.

Rock. Trap.

Danger.

Time to pull it together, Amira.

"I bet we can see what's on the other side," I said, grabbing the flashlight and rushing to the other side of the room. Dax followed at a more leisurely pace. I shone the flashlight through the hole, but I wasn't able to see much other than more of the same stone on the other side.

"What if it's another doorless chamber?" I worried as Dax stepped up behind me. He put one of his sturdy hands on my shoulder.

"Then we'll break through it the same way we did this one," Dax assured me. "Don't touch it, the acid is still active."

"What about food?" I asked. I hadn't eaten since that morning. My stomach was already starting to feel hollow. Dax took a something small and silvery out of his pack and tossed it to me. It was a ration bar.

"We're all set with food." He grinned, obviously recovered from our interlude.

"What about the others?" Now that my mind was clear, I didn't like not knowing where they were. Finding them was going to be a pain. They could be anywhere.

"I'm sure Tu'ver has enough food for them, too," Dax chuckled. "Relax a bit. There's no point in getting worked up when we can't control anything." He walked back across the room and sat down with his back against the wall, facing the disintegrating doorway. After a few moments of hesitation, I joined him.

Before long, I struggled to keep my eyes open. Dax turned off the flashlight and I allowed myself to doze off in the darkness, secure in his arm around me.

DAXION

When I woke to yet more darkness, Amira was still snuggled fast asleep on my shoulder.

I listened to her breathing, felt her heat on my skin. So light, I could barely feel her weight.

Such a small thing to change so much of my world.

Slowly, I extended my free arm and felt around for the flashlight, carefully shining it near Amira's face. I shone it toward the thinner part of the wall, where I'd shot my bolt. I was pleased to find that there was now a hole in the wall big enough for Amira to get through.

"Amira," I whispered, giving her a gentle nudge. She sighed softly and buried her face into my chest. My arm tightened around her, as if by habit, like we always slept this way.

For a change, her face was open, relaxed. All those

worries and fears that tied her into knots seemed to have left her for now.

Reluctantly, I tried again. "Amira," I kissed the top of her head. "Want to get out of here?"

She cracked one eye open.

"How long were we asleep?" she asked.

"I'm not sure," I replied, helping her sit up. She stretched her arms over her head. Her shoulders and elbows made that alarming popping noise again.

"Are you sure you're well?"

"Yes." She looked confused by my question.

"If you say so." I wasn't convinced. "We can get through the wall now." I was going to offer to help her through, but she was on her feet before I could say anything. Excitement shone in her eyes.

"There isn't any leftover toxin on the stone, right?" she asked, casting a wary glance at the hole in the wall. "I don't want to accidentally brush up against it."

"Not at this point," I replied. That didn't appear to put her at ease. "Go through, you'll be fine. Have a little trust."

"Famous last words," she muttered before shimmying through. Once on the other side, she turned around and peered back towards me. "That was a tight squeeze for me. I don't know how you're going to fit, unless you plan on disintegrating more of the wall."

"Let me worry about that." I pressed my palm

against the jagged edge then threw my weight against it. Another few inches of stone fell to the floor. I repeated the process until the hole was wide enough for me to go through, though I still had to duck.

"That's one way to do it." Amira looked stunned. I caught her gaze flicker to my arms before returning to my face. She blushed and looked away.

"Where do you think we are?" I asked, slowly panning the flashlight around. There was something off about the way my voice carried. In a room this spacious, there should have been an echo.

There wasn't.

I wondered if Amira noticed too.

"It's difficult to say." Her delicate brow furrowed. "There's nothing here that would indicate the function of the room, at least, not to me."

I didn't have much of an idea either. It was constructed of the same black stone as the cell we'd fallen into, except here it was ribboned with glowing bands of green, blue, purple, and white. I stepped closer to the wall and gently touched one of the bands. It felt like the grainy surface of a rock, whereas the black stone felt smooth like glass.

Other than the glowing mineral bands, there was nothing else remarkable about the room. It was completely empty.

"Are you disappointed?" I asked Amira. She pursed her lips as she considered her answer.

"No," she said at last. "This place is amazing. It's just unusual for there to be no trace of *anything*. I wasn't expecting a perfectly preserved sitting room or laboratory. Maybe just a few interesting piles of rubble here and there."

"I can make rubble if you want." I shoved at the edge of the jagged hole and a few more chunks of stone broke off. It had the desired effect. Amira laughed.

"I'll come back in five thousand years and I promise I'll find that rubble fascinating."

"We'll be here for five thousand years if we don't find the others," I replied. I hoped they were all right, wherever they were, but Tu'ver was as good at getting out of tough situations as I was, if not better. If he'd fallen into a similar trap, I was confident he'd already found a way out.

"Which way should we go?" Amira asked. Three hallways lead out of the room we stood in, all lined with veins of glowing minerals. From where I stood, they were indistinguishable from each other.

"They were ahead of us, but more on our right when we all fell," I said. "So, let's go to the right."

"That logic is flimsy," Amira hesitated. "Really, really flimsy."

"Do you have a better theory?" I asked, genuinely curious.

Amira pondered for a moment before shaking her head, the nervous, self-questioning look back haunting her eyes.

"At least we're together," I tried to reassure her, anything to make that go away.

"I'll let you know if I need you to crash through a wall." She laughed it off but I could tell she felt better.

We followed the hallway that would put us to the right of the room we'd just escaped from. The glowing bands created a mesmerizing effect, as if the walls were very slightly wavering.

It was nearly impossible to see where another corridor branched off until we were right at the junction. Quite disorienting.

"Have any other plans for five thousand years for now?" I asked.

"What?" She looked confused.

"You said you'd come study the rubble I left behind five thousand years from now. Do you have a secret plan for living that long?" It was unlikely. Okay, impossible. But my time around Axion and Sakev had shown me the value of nonsense, just to get a laugh.

"No," Amira chuckled. "Though, if I did, it would make my job much easier. Humans live for about one hundred years, give or take."

"That's about the same for us," I gestured to my skin.

"What else is the same between our species?" Amira murmured. "Actually, I'd rather ask about the differences," she corrected herself hastily.

I wondered if she was thinking about our kiss last night. I certainly had been.

"There's certainly more than a few things."

"Like what?"

"Nearly all Valorni are vegetarian," I said. I chuckled lightly at the look of surprise on Amira's face.

"That can't be true. I've seen tons of Valorni eating meat in the mess hall," she protested.

"You're right, but that wouldn't be the case if we were on our home planet," I said.

"Why not?" she asked.

"Nearly every creature on Valorn is toxic in some way," I explained. "We can't eat any of the animals. They can't eat us, either."

"So, if I were to take a bite out of you, I would die?" Amira asked.

"I don't know if you would die. I'm not sure if my flesh is compatible with the human digestive system or not." Amira made a face.

"Let's not test it," she said before moving on. "Alright, here's another. I've noticed that there were no Valorni women on the *Vengeance*. Is there a reason for that?"

"Valorni have one of the largest armies in the galaxy," I began. "Nearly every citizen, male or female, serves. However, only the males go into space."

"That doesn't seem right." Amira lifted a brow. "Why shouldn't the females be able to travel through space?"

"The female Valorni excel at protecting the home planet," I explained. "Once a female Valorni bears children, and sometimes earlier, if they have younger siblings, they produce a hormone that increases their territorial tendencies by tenfold. A Valorni woman protecting her homestead is a sight to see and it's also something you don't want to be on the wrong end of."

"And the males don't produce this hormone?" she asked.

"Not that exact one," I replied. "Though don't get me wrong, we're extremely territorial as well. Just not always about land."

"So, the females protect the land and the males protect the skies?" Amira clarified.

"Exactly." I grinned. "Females also take on the responsibility of educating and training our young until they enlist in a military program. Though that's not due to any hormone. They're just very good at it. The running joke among my people is that the planet belongs to the women."

"That sounds like my kind of planet," Amira snorted.

"Valorni women are not fond of other species, but I

think they would admire your spirit." I gave her arm a gentle nudge. She looked down at the floor, but I could still see her grin.

"Is that why Axtin took to Leena right away? Because she was spirited?"

"I believe so," I agreed. "But I'm not going to ask either of them for details."

"That makes sense." She nodded. "So, you were first trained by a Valorni female?"

I nodded proudly. "My mother oversaw my training personally, as well as the training of several other youngsters in my town," I explained. "She was a fearsome female. Once I saw her rip out the tusks of a Molluch with a single hand."

"A what?" Amira looked up at me with a curious expression.

"It's like..." I struggled to put it into terms that she'd understand. "A scaly pig? That's a farm animal from Earth, right?"

"That's right," Amira confirmed. I was proud of myself for remembering. I'd taken it upon myself to learn a bit about humans since we'd crashed down on this planet. "So, a scaly pig with tusks?"

"Yes, and make it ten feet tall." I answered. Amira's eyes widened.

"I can't imagine living on the same planet as something like that," she murmured.

"You live on a planet with walking trees and a slew of other awful creatures," I laughed. Most of the creatures I'd encountered thus far were masters of camouflage. I felt like I was always at a disadvantage.

My mother would have insisted that a challenging fight meant a more rewarding victory.

I'd just rather a few less plants trying to kill us.

Amira looked up at me and opened her mouth like she was about to ask more, but a sound caught our attention.

"That sounds like people arguing," she whispered. Despite the strange way sound carried in these ruins, I guessed they weren't far away.

"I wager it's Tu'ver and the others," I said.

"Hurry up, then!" She grabbed my hand and took off running down the hallway, tugging me behind her despite my longer stride.

I followed, hoping we were ready for whatever else this labyrinth had to throw at us.

No matter what, it wouldn't be getting Amira.

AMIRA

We took two wrong turns. At one point, I was so sure I could hear Mariella's voice on my right side I stumbled blindly down a corridor without looking. The floor gave way and I would've plummeted to my death if Dax hadn't grabbed me at the last minute.

"They've got to be that way." Dax jerked his head in the only direction we'd yet to go.

I couldn't hear the voices anymore. I was beginning to think I'd imagined them entirely.

We rounded the bend and found the others had set up a makeshift camp in a small antechamber off the main hallway. As soon as Mariella saw me, she let out a delighted shriek and ran towards us. When she reached me, she threw her arms around me, wrapping me up in the sort of hug I'd only ever gotten from my mother.

I was frozen at first. She'd caught me off guard. Eventually, I had enough sense to hug her back. I had been worried about her, after all, and was glad to see she was still in one piece.

"I've been worried like crazy!" Mariella exclaimed. "All of Zan's tech is going berserk down here. Tu'ver wanted to see if he could fix it, but Zan won't let him touch anything." Mariella's exasperated sigh told me that the argument had made up the majority of their conversation since we were separated.

"You don't understand tech the way I do," Zan argued. Tu'ver's patience was reaching its breaking point.

"I don't understand tech?" he repeated. "Look at my arms, I *am* tech."

"I'll see if I can sort this out," Dax offered.

"Good luck," Mariella sighed.

"Urai technology is light years ahead of K'ver's," Zan argued. "It's more likely you'll just break it, and then where would we be?"

"Exactly where we are now," Tu'ver replied. I wondered if Zan would be more accommodating if he knew he was arguing with one of the deadliest soldiers on the *Vengeance*.

"What happened when you fell through the trap door?" I turned my attention back to Mariella, confident Dax would have everything well in hand in no time.

"Oh, it was such a mess!" Mariella exclaimed. "We fell into what I assumed was some sort of holding cell, but it had collapsed in on itself. It took us forever to move the rubble. Whatever stone this place is made of is so heavy. Tu'ver did most of the work." Mariella snuck a side-eyed glace at Zan, who was too engrossed in the argument to pay attention to anything else.

"It's a wonder the whole thing didn't come down right on your head," I gasped. The scans from Fen's satellite had shown a few dilapidated areas. I hoped we wouldn't have to go through too many of those. I would hate for this to become my tomb.

"That's exactly why we put some distance between ourselves and the rubble before settling down to camp," Mariella agreed. "Tu'ver figured if we stayed in one place, you'd be more likely to find us than if we all kept wandering. We tried to do a few scouting missions, but it's impossible to judge distance in this place. The nearest turn in any direction is much farther down than it looks." Mariella gestured down the hall. Far away on the other end, I could see the strange glowing mineral bands turn sharply to the left.

"It doesn't look too far," I commented.

"The lines are deceptive," Mariella warned. "I think they were shaped like that on purpose to create an optical illusion. "

"So, we have a hidden entrance, trap doors, rooms designed to be inescapable, and walls that trick the eye," I listed. "It sounds like whoever built this place took some serious precautions. But why?"

"We'll know as soon as we get the tech fixed," Mariella replied.

"*If* we get the tech fixed," I corrected. I snuck a peek over my shoulder at Dax and the others. Tu'ver and Dax were both facing Zan with their arms crossed over their chests, but Zan didn't look the least bit intimidated.

"You've got to admire his dedication," Mariella offered.

"Do I?"

Mariella laughed in response.

"I meant to ask earlier," she continued. "How did you and Dax get out of the trap? Was it collapsed like ours was?"

"No, we dissolved the wall with acid." I enjoyed the Mariella's shocked expression more than I'd care to admit. "Did you see anything interesting when you got out of the trap?"

"No, and that's the interesting part," Mariella

explained. "It's not a surprise that there's no sign of any active inhabitants, but I haven't seen a sign of anything ever living here. I don't think it was built to be lived in."

"The scans from the satellite showed this place to be massive," I mused. "Why would it be so big if it wasn't meant to contain some sort of population? A temple, maybe?"

"Your guess is as good as mine," Mariella shrugged.

"Good news!" Dax called to us. "Zan came to his senses and let Tu'ver work on the equipment. Everything's working even better than it was before."

"How did you convince Zan?" I asked. Dax's reply was a big, toothy grin. I decided not to inquire further. Some secrets were meant to stay that way, right?

"I'm going to use the sonic mapping device." Zan held up a square black screen with a row of small buttons and knobs on the bottom and an antenna sticking out of the top.

"How does it work?" I asked.

"It emits a high-pitched frequency and relies on echolocation to build an image of the overall structure. It will be more detailed than the images retrieved from Fen's satellite." I thought I heard a touch of smugness in his voice.

Zan powered on the device. Piece by piece, I watched lines and angles appear on the screen.

"It will be a few minutes," Zan explained. "This place is quite expansive."

"How many minutes, exactly?" Dax asked, looking uncomfortable and wincing every few seconds.

"I don't have an exact time," Zan replied, not looking up from the scanner.

"Are you okay, Dax?" I asked.

"The frequency he's using is extremely annoying." Dax gave his head a shake as if it would dislodge the sound.

"I don't hear a thing," I replied.

"The frequency chosen is out of the Urai's hearing range. I'm not sure about any other species," Zan said in a matter-of-fact tone.

"Apparently, it's within mine." Dax pressed his fingertips against his temples. "You can add that to our list of differences."

"Hang on," I said. I swung my pack onto the floor and started rifling through its contents. "I might have something that will help." It took dumping nearly everything out of my pack to find what I was looking for. I handed Dax a set of earplugs. Originally, I'd brought them to sleep on the shuttle, but somehow hadn't needed them.

Dax took the tiny clear package and looked at me with a perplexed expression.

"Put them in your ears," I instructed. He did as he

was told. When they were in place, he looked just as confused as he did before. "Do they help at all?" I asked.

"No." He shook his head, speaking louder than normal. I couldn't help but laugh. "I appreciate the gesture, though. Why are you laughing?"

"Because you're yelling in a silent hallway," I giggled. Dax pulled one of the earplugs out of his ear.

"What?" he shouted. Mariella and I doubled over laughing. Dax quickly removed the other earplug and tossed them over his shoulder.

"What odd things you humans do," he grumbled. The only indicator that Zan was still running his scanner was the grimace fixed on Dax's face.

Suddenly, Dax let out a huge sigh and dropped his hands from his temples.

"All done?" I asked.

"It feels like my head was swarmed by Grendles," Dax groaned.

"What the hell is a Grendle?" I asked, against my better judgment.

"It's a small furry creature with sharp little nails and half-inch fangs. Groups hunt together in the thousands. They swarm their prey and strip it down to the bone in minutes," Dax explained.

"I regret asking," I shuddered.

"My scans appear to be incomplete." Zan paced the corridor briskly.

"Do not tell me you have to do it again," Dax growled.

"No," Zan replied. "I am going to try a few different scans to get the most complete picture possible."

"So, the sonic scan wasn't necessary?" Dax asked through clenched teeth.

"I prefer to do my job as thoroughly as possible, so yes it was." Zan paced back and forth a few more times.

"I'm going to break all of his toys," Dax muttered.

"Easy, tiger," I smirked.

"What?" Dax gave me the same perplexed expression he'd given me when I handed him the earbuds.

"Tigers were a big Earth cat. They had stripes too," I explained, pointing to the deep purple bands crossing his arms.

"Are they anything like Grendles?"

"Not in the slightest," I replied.

"Then I will take that as a compliment," Dax smiled.

"Amira, have a look at this, will you?" Zan called to me. I hurried over and examined the screen Zan was showing me. The scan of the structure looked far more complete than the one we'd gotten off the satellite, but in the center of it was a pulsing blob of green.

"What's that?" I asked, peering closer.

"It's an immense power signature," Zan explained. "And, from the look of things, it's directly in the center of the ruins."

"That can't be a coincidence." Excitement bubbled through me. Something was stored away in these ruins, something powerful.

"Well, everyone," I clapped my hands together. "I believe we have our target."

DAXION

"We can see it on the screen," Amira muttered. "Why can't we get there?"

She sat in a corner of the latest bare room, checked the satellite scans again, and mumbled under her breath about how things shouldn't be so empty.

I turned to the others. "Does anyone have an idea?" Tu'ver shook his head, as did Mariella. Zan looked at his own scans.

"It is a perplexing situation," he said as he looked up. "Perhaps this was built and before it could be inhabited, the denizens were forced to leave."

It was an interesting theory, but wouldn't make Amira happy and didn't get us any closer to our target. "We've been searching for more than an hour, and all we've found are more hallways, more empty rooms, more frustration, and no way to get to that power source. Any suggestions?" I asked.

Tu'ver spoke up. "I suggest we find our way out soon. We have limited supplies and I don't see a pathway to that power source in the center."

Zan agreed with him.

"Let's go another hour, then make our way out," I decided.

The others nodded, and I went to break it to Amira. She wasn't happy, but even she admitted that running low on supplies couldn't be avoided.

"One hour left. Any direction you pick," I promised.

She chose yet another pathway that might lead towards the center of the ruins and we proceeded that way.

Tu'ver led the way, maybe a dozen paces ahead of us, but after only a few minutes, stopped short and let out a curse that would have made Axtin proud.

As the rest of us made our way forward, Tu'ver broke a piece of the glowing wall off and dropped it in front of him.

It fell for a very long time.

There was a hole in the ground, and based on Zan's calculations, it extended well over three thousand feet down.

"Well, that's just fun," Mariella said. "Now what?"

"The only way left to the center of the ruins that the

scans project, is across that hole," Amira said. "How far across is it?"

Zan tapped on his tech board with a flurry of fingers, then looked back at Amira. "Approximately twenty-five of your feet."

"Oh." Amira looked scared. As I looked down the hole and imagined what it would be like to fall down it, Tu'ver flew past me and landed on the other side. He looked back at us and shrugged, a small grin on his face.

"Apparently we're going that way," I said.

"What do you mean, we're going that way? I can't make that jump," Amira said.

I smiled at her in an attempt to calm her. "It's okay, watch." I looked at Mariella, and she must have known my idea, because she swallowed hard and nodded. I gently grabbed hold of her and threw her across the chasm. Tu'ver caught her easily and as he set her down, she kissed his cheek.

"Next!" Tu'ver called across.

I looked at Amira, but she backed away a couple of steps, shaking her head. I shrugged and looked at Zan.

"I will not be thrown like some insignificant child. There must be a better way across," he said with some actual venom in his speech pad's robotic voice.

I wasn't in the mood for games or arguments, however. "It's simple, Zan. Either I throw you across, or you jump across. Unless your tech can somehow turn itself into a bridge, there's no other way." As I spoke, I stepped closer to him, keeping my hands at my sides.

Zan shook his head and brought his hand to the speech pad. I snapped my arms out and grabbed him, spun around and threw him across to Tu'ver. Tu'ver caught him easily and set him down nearly as quickly.

"See?" I said with a smile. I turned my attention to Amira and held my hands out to her. "You'll be okay," I said calmly.

She shook her head with fervor. "No. What if you don't throw me right? What if he doesn't catch me? What if I get twisted around and come up short? No. No." She kept shaking her head as she backed away from me.

"Amira," I kept my voice calm. "Look at your map, there's no other way over. This is our only direction."

"But...but...what, wha-what if..." she stammered. I could see that she was terrified.

I understood her fear, the thought of falling that far down wasn't my idea of a great way to die.

"Alright, sweetheart. I won't throw you," I promised.

She stopped backing away. "You...won't...throw me?" she asked, eyes narrowed. "I was right here when you snuck up on Zan, remember?"

"I promise."

"Then...how?"

I looked at her and held out my arms. "Climb up," I

said. "I'll hold onto you as I jump across. Valorni are better at jumping than K'ver are, and you saw how easy it was for Tu'ver to make it."

She looked behind her, back down at the tablet, then past me before she finally nodded. "Okay," she said with a shaky voice. She came to me and wrapped her arms around me as I picked her up.

"Hold on tight," I whispered to her as I turned around. "Here we go!" Tu'ver, Mariella, and Zan moved aside, pressing themselves against the walls as I ran. I pumped my legs hard as I reached the edge in only a few strides.

I planted my foot and jumped, cold air around us as we flew, clearing the hole with ease.

What I hadn't counted on was our combined weight landing quite so heavily on the other side.

For a substance that had been so solid when we wanted to break through, it now shattered beneath my feet with alarming speed.

My stupid grin changed in a hurry as loud cracking noises filled the air.

"RUN!" Tu'ver yelled.

We sprinted as the floor behind us fell away, tumbling loudly down into nothingness. As we ran, we turned three corners before running into a dead-end.

Amira, still clinging to me, yelled over the noise,

"This isn't supposed to be here! It's supposed to be a straight passage."

"Look," Mariella pointed. "Up there!" Several yards above us was a ledge and an opening. "We need to climb!"

"How?" Amira said. I thought for a second while Tu'ver yelled that the passageway was breaking faster.

Then I had an idea.

"Hold on," I said to Amira as I swung her around onto my back. As she grabbed on tightly, I reached into my quiver and pulled out two bolts. I jammed them into the wall at different heights, then pulled out two more bolts. I climbed up, jamming bolts in as I went to create a sort of ladder for the others to follow. A quick look down showed Tu'ver as the last to climb.

When we reached the ledge, I pulled myself and Amira up and over. She let go of me and rolled away as I went back to help Mariella over the edge. Next was Zan, struggling to make it up with the straps of his tech crossing his chest, threatening to tangle him. I reached down and grabbed him, yanking him up the last little bit. Tu'ver was the last to come up, bringing my bolts with him as he did. I helped him over the edge and we all backed away as the passageway below us fell away with thunderous crashes.

When the sound finally stopped, we all looked at one another.

Everyone was breathing hard and Mariella shook in Tu'ver's arms. Zan's eyes were closed and he held his hands pressed against his head.

I picked up the bolts and returned them to my quiver, then looked at the others.

"Well, I don't know about the rest of you, but I'm hungry," I panted. "Anyone else?" I forced my breathing to slow down and tried to calm down my racing heartbeat. I felt and heard my own heartbeat in my ears, that was how fast and hard it was pounding.

"Really?" Mariella asked sarcastically.

"Well," I shrugged. "I'm either hungry or 'scared shitless' as you humans say, so I went with hungry."

Mariella fought back a chuckle and lost, which caused Amira to chuckle. Soon, all of us, not counting Zan, were laughing uncontrollably.

"I don't see what is so humorous about our situation," he said through his pad. The robotic voice didn't help, and we all laughed even harder. Somewhere in the middle of the laughter I heard him say, "Ah, I understand now. Lesser species coping mechanism."

I knew he was insulting us, but I also saw his own shoulders jostle up and down a bit, so he found it funny, too.

"Does anyone know what time of day it is?" Amira managed to ask between gasps.

Zan answered by holding up his tablet. It was late evening.

"Already?" Mariella asked. "We've been down here that long?"

"Being underground changes all perceptions of time," Tu'ver answered. "While you feel that it hasn't been long at all, I feel as though a year of my life has already passed. I'm honestly surprised that it's only evening."

"So, what do we do?" I asked. "Do we search a little longer, or do we rest here? We've still got time on that hour."

Amira and Mariella raised their hands and spoke at the same time, "All good for resting here." They looked at one another and burst out with another round of laughter.

As they laughed, I looked at Tu'ver and Zan.

"If we're careful, we've got enough supplies for another day or so. I don't think we'll be heading back the same way, anyhow," I said.

Whatever plans we had made, it seemed the structure had some ideas of its own.

AMIRA

His hands whispered over my skin. Goosebumps covered me from my neck down to my toes. Every nerve in my body was attuned to his movements.

A large, rough hand crept up my shirt and played with one of my breasts while the other hand ventured down and –

I jolted awake with a gasp. I looked to my right, so sure I was going to find Dax beside me.

He wasn't there.

Of course he wasn't.

I realized now that I'd been dreaming. It was so real. Even now I could still feel his imagined hand dancing over my skin.

My breath hitched as a thin layer of sweat coated my forehead. My hair was damp underneath me. A dull ache throbbed between my legs as I struggled to separate the dream from reality. After a few minutes of tossing and turning in discomfort, I gave up. I wiggled my way out of my sleeping sack as silently as I could manage. Mariella slept not five feet away from me. Her breathing was slow and steady.

A walk would clear my head. I wouldn't go far. I was well aware of how easy it was to get lost in this labyrinth. At least from here, there was only one direction for me to go.

We'd set up camp a little way back from the ledge that marked where the wall gave out earlier today. Tu'ver, Dax, and Zan were confident the part of the structure we were in would hold, but the idea of it still made me uneasy.

Dax had been so kind when he helped me across the gap in the path.

I think, if something like that were to happen again, it'd be easy to trust him to keep me safe. I'd joked earlier about the number of times he was going to save my ass.

I now believed the answer he gave me.

I'd believe anything he said, maybe.

I walked farther down the corridor, letting my hand trail along a stripe of pale blue. I stretched onto the tips of my toes to keep my hand on it when the stripe curved up.

The different colored stripes had to mean something. Their design was too precise to be random. My only theory, so far, was that the lines served as a map. Follow the blue bands one way, the purple another, and so on.

But that didn't make much sense considering the only thing of note in this entire place was whatever was causing that power surge in the center.

I came to a fork in the corridor. I could go right or carry on straight ahead. I decided to go right, but wouldn't take any other turn I came across. I'd get lost otherwise. I kept walking with my fingers brushing the wall, trailing by my hip to keep me oriented.

Suddenly, the support dropped out from under my hand.

A small alcove was cut into the wall. When I backed up, then traced the opening, I'd guess it was only four feet high and less than a foot deep.

I took a few more steps back. I was only feet away but could no longer see the alcove, thanks to the camouflaging abilities of the glowing bands.

How many little alcoves like this had we missed?

I knelt down and peered into the alcove. I wished I'd brought a flashlight or something.

While the glowing bands gave enough light in the passage to see, within this separate space, it was entirely dark.

At first glance, there appeared to be nothing in the alcove at all. I ran my hand along the walls just to make sure I wasn't missing anything. Perhaps I'd find a hidden door, like I had in the trap. If I did, I hoped I wouldn't have to use Dax's toxic bolts to break through it.

It'd been necessary at the time, but I hated the idea of destroying any piece of a structure that had been standing for who knows how long.

After a few minutes of searching, I was ecstatic when my fingers brushed across a series of shallow gouges in the stone. I moved as close as I could get and squinted against the glowing light from the colored bands.

I could make out three vertical lines about two inches tall and carved about a quarter of an inch deep into the stone. Next to it were more lines of varying height. Every once in a while, there were horizontal lines cutting across others. A handful of times, I found a perfectly circular indent.

I quickly ruled them out as decorative. They were so difficult to see, I doubted they were placed for ornamentation.

Writing?

I wanted to squeal with excitement, but I didn't want to wake the others. The possibilities were endless what they could be.

Questions fired off in my head one after another faster than I could come up with theories to answer them.

A shuffling sound came from behind me. I scrambled to my feet, nearly banging my head on the lip of the alcove. My hands clenched into fists, ready to fight.

"Easy."

Dax. My sigh of relief was audible.

"You scared the daylights out of me," I scolded.

"I wasn't trying to." I could see Dax's brilliant smile, even in the low light. My dream came flooding back to me, as did the heat to my face.

"What are you doing here?" I looked away. Already, I could feel my heart beating faster.

"I saw you get up and walk away from camp. I followed you. It's far too easy to get lost in a place like this," Dax replied.

"And what if we both get lost?" I arched a brow.

"That wouldn't be so bad, would it?" Dax shrugged. "At least you wouldn't be wandering around by yourself." He stepped closer to me, then noticed the alcove. "Ah, I see you've found something." He crouched down to have a look for himself. I knelt beside him.

"There are markings in the wall," I explained. I took his hand in mine and led it to the engravings. "Feel here."

"What do you think they are?" he asked.

"My guess is it's some sort of writing but I don't know the language," I explained. "Does it feel familiar to you?"

"Not at all. Zan might know. He's supposed to be our expert on these things."

"I'm just grateful for something to study. I feel rather useless." I tugged my bottom lip between my teeth.

"You're the reason we found all of this in the first place. You're far from useless." He took his hand away from the wall and brought it to my cheek.

His touch surprised me. My first instinct was to pull away, but I suppressed it. I didn't want to pull away from him.

Not from him, not ever.

The way the bands of colored light shone against his deep green skin made him look almost iridescent, like someone pulled straight out of the old myths of lost Earth.

I remembered my dream again. Every sensation rushed back to me as my breath quickened.

His eyes searched my face. His gaze came to rest on my parted lips.

"Dax," I sighed. That was all the invitation he needed.

His mouth crashed into mine as one strong hand snaked into my hair.

"I can't get you out of my mind," he said between kisses. "It's wrong of me to feel this way when I'm in charge of protecting you, but I can't help it."

"I can't get you out of my mind, either," I confessed. "Not even when I sleep." Never mind violating some stupid code of conduct likely set in place by General Rouhr. He wasn't here, so to hell with it.

His tongue darted against the seam of my lips, demanding, urging. I opened to him, gasping at the penetration as our tongues danced, exploring each other. He pressed me against him, urgent caresses ensuring I felt every inch of him, hard between us.

Dax kissed me until my lips felt achy and swollen, then kissed and nipped down my neck, back to the shell of my ear, and back down again, every touch setting my nerves on fire.

He sank to the floor, kneeling with my legs straddling his, as his strong hands kneaded my back, working their way under my shirt to tease the undersides of my breasts.

Leaning forward, he forced me back until I rested nearly flat, supported entirely by his hands.

"Just relax," he instructed, his voice a low, hungry growl.

Dazed by the onslaught of sensations, I did as I was told.

Flat on my back, I gazed up at the crisscrossing patterns of light on the walls and ceiling. It looked like the tails of a thousand comets suspended in time.

As if I were made of spun glass, he lowered me to the floor, loosed my boots from my feet. Hooking his thumbs under the waistline of my pants, he pulled them down, along with my undergarments, in one swift motion. Chills ran the length of my body when my bare skin touched the cold surface of the stone floor, lost in the heat sparked with every touch.

He kissed up from my ankles to my thighs, occasionally nipping gently at my skin. When he finally reached the apex of my thighs, my body screamed in anticipation.

The first gentle, tentative stroke of his tongue almost had me completely undone. A shuddering gasp tore from my mouth. I arched my back against the stone floor, lifting my hips forward in a silent plea for more.

Dax's laugh was closer to a growl as he took my hint.

I wound my hands into his hair as he devoured me. I allowed myself to drown in the blissful sensation. When his clever tongue found my sensitive nub, I cried out. He narrowed in on that spot, licking and sucking until I thrashed, helpless beneath him.

His hands gripped my hips to hold me steady, keep me open for his delicious attentions.

Streaks of electric pleasure shuddered through me and stars exploded behind my closed eyelids. Trembling, my legs clamped together of their own accord, but no match for his strength as he held me open.

I cried out once more, lifting my entire upper body off the floor as wave after wave crashed over me. When I was finally spent, I could hardly sit myself upright. Dax lay beside me, idly caressing one thigh, surveying his handiwork. The wicked gleam in his eyes told me he was pleased.

"I think it's time we got you back to camp so you can get a proper sleep." He tucked a wild strand of hair behind my ear.

"I don't think I can move." My voice was soft and breathy. Dax laughed and pulled me close to him.

"We'll sleep here then," he decided, pulling me on top of his chest. "All the better in case I decide I need to taste you again."

"Please do," I grinned.

DAXION

One of the many downsides to being trapped in these ruins was that without a tablet or other device, it was impossible to determine the time.

I hoped we slept for a while. Amira needed the rest. At the moment, she was still fast asleep with her head on my chest, no worry held in her brow or displeasure hidden at the corners of her mouth.

This was how she should always look.

I'd do my best to make it so.

I woke her as gently as I could. As much as I would've liked to wait for her to wake up naturally, I feared we didn't have that kind of time to spare. The longer it took us to get to the center of the ruins, the more time the Xathi had to catch up with us.

And the more our supplies would dwindle.

"Good morning," she murmured without opening her eyes.

"Good morning to you," I replied. "I hate to wake you, but we should get back to the others."

"I wonder if they've noticed we're missing." She sat up slowly. Her bones did that horrible cracking thing that apparently human bones do.

Amira could insist it was normal all she wanted, but I had my doubts.

"I don't think so," I decided. "They'd be looking for us if they'd noticed. We aren't far from camp either. So, if they were looking, they would've found us by now."

"Unless they went the wrong way." A crease appeared between her brows.

And the worry was back.

Once she was off me completely, I got to my feet. My neck and my right arm were a bit stiff after sleeping in that position all night but it was nothing I couldn't manage. A few stretches would take care of it.

I was far more worried about Amira. She groaned when I helped her to her feet.

"Are you all right?" I asked.

"I feel like I've run twenty miles," she moaned. I couldn't resist it.

"You're welcome."

I received a light flick on the arm in response.

"It's from sleeping on the floor," she insisted with a wink.

"Whatever you say."

When we made our way back to camp, we found that the others were already awake and packed up.

"At least we don't have to worry about them being lost searching for us," I murmured to Amira.

"They must've known we were close by," she whispered back.

"They're back from their little field trip!" Mariella chirped when she saw us. I didn't know what she meant, but Amira flushed red.

Tu'ver walked over with a smug look on his face. "I trust your little excursion was pleasurable," he emphasized the last word more than necessary. Far more than necessary.

"It was productive," Amira said defensively. She'd started to fidget with her hands.

"Sounded like it," Mariella teased.

"No," Amira rolled her eyes. "I mean we found something."

Their expressions shifted rapidly.

"What did you find?" Tu'ver asked.

"Writing, I think."

Zan materialized at her side, clearly interested. "Take me to it," he demanded. "Perhaps, I can identify the origins of these structures."

"That's exactly what I was hoping to hear." Amira was smiling again.

Eagerly, she led Zan back to the secret alcove. I followed behind with Mariella and Tu'ver.

"Incredible," Zan said after a few moments. "I am quite certain we are standing in a structure built by the Aeryx."

"Who are they?" Amira asked.

"I've never heard of them," Tu'ver said.

"I haven't either," I replied. "They must not have lived in our galaxy."

"You would be surprised how far-flung this species is." Zan pulled a small black case from his pack and opened it.

Amira's face lit up, though the case looked like it contained nothing more than a few oddly shaped picks and brushes. "I need to clean the markings for scanning. I have seen very little dust here, but any may alter the results. Amira, would you like to do it?"

Amira nodded eagerly and knelt down beside Zan.

"What are you scanning them for?" she asked. Amira selected a short silver-handled brush topped with a poof of soft round bristles.

Zan supplied her with a small tube of clear liquid, likely water, and she dampened the brush.

"I have something that can translate nearly any written language," Zan replied. "Thankfully, a handful of Aeryx writing samples have been found before, so we will not be completely left to our own devices."

Now it was Mariella whose expression lit up with interest. She knelt down behind Amira, who was now all the way into the alcove.

"I think Zan might steal them both out from under us if we're not careful," Tu'ver jested. "Though, from what I heard last night, I don't think you have anything to worry about."

"Don't let Amira hear you," I warned him with a laugh. "She looked ready to skin you alive earlier."

"That's odd." Amira's voice pulled my attention away from Tu'ver. She'd pulled herself out of the alcove and was holding the brush up for Zan to see. The bristles were still pristine white.

"What is it?" I asked.

"There would usually be debris, dead insect, mineral build up, or at least some dust. But these markings are as if someone had cleaned them hours ago." She passed the brush back to Zan, who put it away.

"That doesn't make sense," Tu'ver replied. "I know this place has been sealed up for ages but at least some sediment from the desert above should have made its way in, especially with the partially collapsed areas."

No dust, no echo.

This place got stranger by the hour.

"At least that means we can get an accurate

translation," Mariella chimed up.

"Quite right." Zan pulled out another device with a thick antenna on one end and a small screen on the other.

"This one doesn't use sound, does it?" I asked.

Amira's shoulders shook with laughter, but she managed to be quiet about it.

Mostly.

"It uses a very sensitive laser," Zan explained as if he'd completely forgotten the incident with the sonic scanner. He shifted his focus to Mariella. "You work with translation, yes?"

"I do," Mariella said proudly.

"I'd let you take over this process, but I don't think you can read Urai." Zan tilted the screen so she could see it. It was covered in markings that were different, but just as unreadable, as those on the wall. We'd only been among the Urai for a short while. The neurotranslators we all wore helped to understand different spoken languages, but the Urai didn't speak. The speech pads they used emitted their dialogue in a language we already knew.

Learning their language would need a different approach. Assuming the Xathi left us time for such academic pursuits.

"No, I can't," Mariella admitted. "But I'd like to watch anyway."

"Once I do the initial translation, I'll convert it into something the rest of you can read," Zan offered. Mariella nodded in gratitude.

Zan powered on the device and a bright green laser shone out. It found the markings and quickly scanned a detailed image onto the screen. Sections of the images on the screen illuminated as Zan started his analysis. Some pieces lit up white, others red. Zan swept the red fragments off to the side and focused on the white.

"It appears that I can pull a partial translation," he announced. "This marking here means gate or doorway. There's another marking here that means guard or protect. This one here is a bit odd, the closest translation would be temple but that's not exact."

"This is a temple?" Amira asked. "Yes!" She pumped her fist in victory.

"Not exactly, but something like it," Zan replied.

"And it's guarded?" Amira continued. Zan nodded, his eyes fixed on the screen.

"These markings imply that this wasn't a place of residence, but a holding chamber of sorts," Zan continued. "The best translation is that this temple contains the Gate to the Universe."

"What the hell is that?" Amira asked, visibly excited.

"It doesn't say. But I would guess that power signature at the center could have something to do with it."

"How literally should we be interpreting these markings?" I wondered out loud.

"Dax makes a good point," Mariella agreed. "This translation is only partial and it's not exact. There could be many ways to interpret it."

"It's possible this was meant to be read poetically," Amira mused. "But without any additional context, it's hard to say for sure."

"They weren't a very poetic people," Zan added. "And they were advanced space travelers, even more so than the Urai. It's not often I can say that about another species. If any species were to possess a literal Gate to the Universe, it would be the Aeryx"

"Weren't?" Amira piped up.

"Yes?" Zan replied.

"It's just that a moment ago, you referred to the Aeryx in the present tense, but now you've switched to past. Why?"

"There's much debate surrounding whether or not the Aeryx have become extinct," Zan explained. "Aeryx finds are few and far between and it's often difficult to accurately determine the age."

"If they aren't extinct, then where could they be?" Amira asked.

"The leading theory is that they've moved to an unknown area of space. There were several instances where the Urai arrived on a planet thought to be undiscovered, only to find traces of the Aeryx," Zan explained.

"Is that what you think?" Amira pressed.

"I think that theory is too optimistic," Zan replied. "After all, this is a race that the Xathi took an active interest in. The Xathi don't have any particular interest in humans and look what they've done to your planet."

There was a heavy moment of silence.

"I apologize. That was careless of me to say," Zan said.

I reached forward and gave Amira a light squeeze on the shoulder.

"No, you're right." Her voice sounded thick but she worked through it. "The Xathi see us as food and fodder. The only thing of interest to them doesn't even belong to us."

"So, you think the Xathi wiped out the Aeryx?"

"I do. But as I said, it's only a theory." Zan packed up his equipment. We'd gotten all the information we could from the alcove.

"Well then," Amira stood up and brushed her hands off. I figured it was more of a habit than anything since there was no dust to knock away. "I suppose we should go find the Gate to the Universe."

"You seem very excited," I grinned at her.

"Of course I am!" She was beaming again. "I've waited my whole life for something like this."

AMIRA

F inally, we had something solid to go on. Granted, it wasn't much, but it was way more than we'd started with.

I wished I'd brought more survey equipment, not that there was much to survey besides a few chips of stone and some marking on the wall.

I'd have given anything to have my nice field camera with me, but I had to leave it behind when the Xathi attacked Kaster.

What I wouldn't give to stumble upon an abandoned dwelling, or city center or laboratory. A burial chamber would make an incredible find, but I didn't want to be morbid. From the translation Zan was able to get, it didn't sound like anyone ever lived here, let alone died here.

"From the way Zan talked about the Aeryx, it doesn't sound like they left behind anything for me to study." Mariella startled me out of my thoughts.

"I was just thinking the same thing," I replied.

"What good is an archivist if there are no archives?" Mariella threw her hands up.

"I'm an archeologist with nothing to dig up. Believe me, I know exactly how you feel," I sympathized.

"If this was a city instead of a temple, imagine what would've been left behind for us to find." Mariella sighed wistfully.

"Did you ever read up on temples on Earth? They were usually filled to the brim with artifacts," I replied.

"Zan did say temple was the closest translation, not an exact one," Mariella reminded me. "Maybe the Aeryx don't mean temples the way the people of Earth used them."

"This place makes me think of that old Greek myth. The one about the labyrinth," I commented.

"You mean the one they tossed prisoners in? There was a monster living in that labyrinth."

"A minotaur," I supplemented.

"I don't want to think about it," Mariella shuddered. "I'll convince myself there's a monster or something hunting the halls and I'll be too jumpy to be useful."

"If there was something stalking us, I'm sure Tu'ver and Dax could handle it," I reassured her.

"I don't doubt that." Mariella looked over her shoulder at Tu'ver and smiled proudly. "But still, I'd rather find a library or an archive instead of a monster."

"It's fun to imagine," I agreed. We walked in a companionable silence for a few strides before I noticed the sly look Mariella was giving me.

"What?'" I asked.

"So...you and Dax?" she gave me a playful nudge.

"What about me and Dax?" I was already blushing.

"Don't play coy!" Mariella admonished. "Especially not after the spectacular sound show we all heard last night."

"Was I really that loud?" I covered my face with my hands. "These stupid corridors don't even echo."

"Exactly," Mariella winked. "And yes, you were really that loud. Not going to lie to you, I was a little bit jealous."

"You have Tu'ver though," I reminded her.

"Yes, I do! But it's not like I could pull him down a corridor and have my way with him when it meant Zan would be left alone," Mariella explained. "So tonight, you and Dax have to babysit Zan so Tu'ver and I can go have some fun."

I didn't know what to say. I wasn't close with many girls growing up. My sister, for whatever her reasons had been, hadn't exactly been around for me to learn from.

This sort of girl-speak was uncharted territory for me.

But sleeping with aliens was also uncharted territory for me.

Apparently, this trip was going to be full of surprises.

"Don't worry," Mariella smiled. "I'm only teasing. Though, I wouldn't mind some alone time with Tu'ver."

"Don't let me stop you," I forced a laugh.

"So, were you and Dax just burning off some stress or are you two more serious than that?" Mariella asked. To her credit, she seemed to genuinely care.

"I'm not sure," I confessed. "We haven't known each other for very long. I feel a connection with him, for sure. I wouldn't be upset if he felt the same way. But like I said, we haven't known each other for long."

"Sometimes it doesn't take long," Mariella explained. "I felt something special the moment I met Tu'ver. I wish I'd done something about it sooner. But, as you can see, everything worked out the way it was meant to."

"I fought with Dax the first time I met him," I frowned. Mariella tipped her head back and laughed.

"That doesn't mean anything! Leena and Axtin fought all the time at first and look at them now." I didn't know Leena or Axtin very well, and I certainly didn't know much about how they got together. "I'm pretty sure your sister wasn't very fond of Vrehx when they first met, either."

"By the time I got to the *Vengeance*, they were sort of friends. He stood up to me for her. He called me ungrateful," I recalled, blushing. To be fair, I *was* being ungrateful. Jeneva and Vrehx had gone to great lengths to save my life.

"My point is that you shouldn't overthink things. Just let them happen." Mariella gave me an encouraging smile.

Letting this happen wasn't my strong suit, but maybe I could give it a shot for Dax.

We walked on as I pondered Mariella's advice, keeping my gaze fixed on the bands of color in the wall.

Suddenly, I noticed a change in their pattern. It was subtle at first but eventually, it was clear some of the bands were altering their course.

I could see a bright spot in the wall a hundred or so yards ahead of us.

"I think there's something up ahead," I called back to the others. We picked up the pace. More lines appeared in the wall, brighter than the others. They all grew brighter as we moved closer to the glowing spot up ahead.

By the time we reached it, I had to raise my hand to block the blinding light, but even what shone around my hand stung my eyes.

"What is it?" Mariella asked.

"No idea," I replied. I turned my head away from the light, but that didn't have any effect. "Can anyone get closer?"

"I'll try," Dax said. His eyes were almost completely shut even though he was using his hands to shield his face. He took one step forward, and the bright light disappeared.

I blinked, trying to adjust to the near darkness once more. I heard a grating noise, like stone against stone.

"What's happening? I can hardly see," I asked.

"The wall's moving," Tu'ver said. "It's separating into cubes and folding in on itself."

"There's only darkness on the other side," Dax added.

Maybe K'ver and Valorni eyes were not as sensitive to drastic light changes as human eyes were, because there was no way I could see anything.

"Is it a secret doorway?" Mariella asked. "Does it go to a hidden chamber?"

"I don't think so." Dax's tone was ominous.

I rubbed my eyes vigorously and strained to see past the spots dancing across my field of vision. At first, I thought my eyes were deceiving me, but I quickly realized they weren't.

Staring at us from within the darkness was a pair of glowing green eyes with black slits for pupils. I barely had time to process that before a great creature of stone leaped out at us.

Tu'ver moved first, grabbing Mariella around the waist and pulling her to safety. Zan bolted in the opposite direction.

The creature looked as if it were made of the same black stone the walls were made of. I could see my reflection in its body as it turned its cold gaze to me. Its body was similar to that of a dog, but the stone formed sharp spikes over its back and shoulders. It exposed its glistening black teeth and crouched, ready to leap.

It lunged forward at me, too fast for me to dodge.

I closed my eyes and waited for the blow, but it never came.

Instead, there was a crash.

Cringing, I risked a peek.

Dax had charged the creature from the side, hard enough to knock it to the ground. Sparks flew off the beast's back as Tu'ver shot at it from a distance, Mariella safely behind him.

"The bullets don't make a difference!" Dax yelled. "They just ricochet off it." Tu'ver took aim once more.

"Hold its head steady!" he called to Dax. Dax grabbed a bolt from his quiver and slid it under the stone creature's head, grabbing it around the neck.

The creature thrashed, but Tu'ver only needed a second.

There was a sound like shattering glass and the creature howled in rage. Tu'ver shot out one of its eyes. It bucked and rolled, taking Dax with it. Dax's left arm slid in between the creature's obsidian teeth.

The black spikes punctured his green skin.

Now it was Dax's turn to howl. With his left arm still trapped in the beast's maw, he clutched the bolt in his right and drove it deep into the creature's remaining eye.

It released its grip on Dax and stumbled.

Dax seized the moment, grabbing the creature on either side of the head and twisting violently.

There was a sickening crack, then the creature's body went limp.

Well, most of it.

Dax held its head in his arms. He tossed it to the side with a look of disgust and it shattered on the floor.

I walked over to him. I didn't realize my hands were shaking until I rested one on his shoulder.

"Are you all right?" he demanded.

"Are you?" I replied.

Tu'ver and Mariella walked over to us. Zan had returned but was keeping his distance.

"Looks like there was a minotaur after all," I said to Mariella. Her face was pale.

"A what?" Dax asked, breathing heavily.

"Don't worry about it," I dismissed. "Let me look at

your arm." A row of puncture wounds dotted his upper arm. I retrieved the disinfectant and bandages from Dax's pack and returned to him.

"I'm sure you know the drill. This will sting a bit," I warned him before pouring the disinfectant over his arm.

"That's the part I hate the most," he laughed through the sting. I carefully wrapped his wounds and planted a gentle kiss over the bandage when I was done.

"Does this count as you saving my ass?" Dax asked. For someone who'd just had a few chunks taken out of his arm, he was in a remarkably good mood.

"Maybe," I shrugged and smiled up at him. "But we're a long way from even."

"I can't wait to see how you make it up to me." He pressed a kiss onto my forehead.

"I'll make it up to you on one condition," I replied. "No more fighting stone monsters."

"I can't make any promises."

DAXION

Amira was my mate.

I was certain of it.

I liked to think I always had the well-being of others in mind, but with her it was different.

Her well-being was all that mattered to me. I'd stop at nothing to ensure that she was safe and happy.

The problem was, I didn't know what to do with this realization. I should probably tell Amira at some point, but the more I thought about it, the less sure I was that telling her was the right course of action.

If I told her, there would always be a chance that she didn't feel the same way. Humans were still such a mystery, and Amira was even more unpredictable.

Our time together, the feel of her in my arms, the feel of her skin... all of that meant something to me.

But what if it didn't to her?

That would hurt, but I'd be able to live with it. I'd still do everything I could to keep her safe. Going into this war, I knew I'd fight my hardest for the cause, but it was different now.

Before, I fought for my family, my team and what they loved.

Now, I'd be fighting for someone I loved. I'd put my life on the line for this planet because it was the right thing to do. Now, I'd lay my life down because it was her planet.

If we survived this war, and if she felt the same way, we could live a long and happy life together. I didn't know how Amira felt on the subject, but I'd always wanted children. Being the oldest of ten, I often cared for my younger siblings. I wasn't just good at it, I liked it, too.

But there were other things to consider.

She was kinder and more thoughtful than most people gave her credit for but she'd only just learned how to open up to people. I worried it might be too much if I started showering her with declarations of love and devotion.

It could be something she wasn't ready for yet. Not to mention the fact that she had only just warmed up to my kind. The last thing I wanted was to scare her off.

Though I didn't imagine Amira was someone who was easily frightened away.

And if our hearts and minds weren't already enough to contend with, there was the Xathi. I might not survive the war. She might not survive the war. If I was ever put in a position where I had to choose between her and my team, could I make that choice, let alone the right choice?

The questions and uncertainty made my head ache.

I needed advice.

"Tu'ver, do you have a minute?"

His response was a clipped nod and I indicated that we should walk farther away from the group than we currently were. "I've recently realized something but I'm not sure what I should do. I know you've been in a similar situation and-"

"You're in love with Amira," he cut me off with a knowing smile.

"Is it that obvious?" I asked.

"It's not a bad thing," he assured me. "I actually think you two are well suited for each other."

"High praise, indeed," I laughed. "You and Mariella do so well together despite the world coming down around you. I want Amira to be my mate, as Mariella is yours, but there's so much uncertainty surrounding the Xathi and the war. Is it a good idea?"

"I think the fact that there's so much uncertainty is what makes forming these kinds of relationships a good idea," Tu'ver answered, scanning the corridor for any threats. "We've seen a lot of terrible things. It lifts the spirit to know there's some kindness waiting for you at home."

"I didn't think of it that way," I mused. "How do you and Mariella deal with knowing that any of these days could be our last?"

"She's funny about it," Tu'ver laughed "She won't even entertain the possibility. Every time I try to talk about it, she laughs and tells me there's no point in worrying about something that won't happen."

"What makes her so sure?" I asked.

"I ask her that all the time. The only answer she gives me is, 'I won't allow it.' She says it with such a cheery conviction that I'm actually starting to believe the universe would bend to her will to keep her happy," Tu'ver chuckled.

"Think she could bend the universe to make the Xathi disappear?" I asked dryly.

"If only," Tu'ver agreed. "I won't lie to you. There is a strain that comes with being in love during a war. I know she worries every time I go out on patrol. I worry whenever she's out of my sight. It does make the time together sweeter, though."

"How do you spend your time together?" I asked.

Tu'ver looked at me with an arched brow and a smirk. "Other than the obvious," I laughed.

"I've found that routine helps combat the chaos," Tu'ver explained. "Once a week we have what Mariella calls 'date night'. I cook something, we have a quiet dinner alone together. We talk about anything and everything."

"That sounds nice," I admitted. "Too bad I'm a horrible cook."

"I still remember the time you were put on galley duty," Tu'ver shuddered.

It wasn't one of my finest moments. I had to be Snipes' assistant cook for the night a few months back. I just about put everyone out of commission with some undercooked meat.

"For Amira's sake, I'll think of something else besides dinner," I laughed.

"In the end, it doesn't matter what you do. It only matters that you both enjoy the time spent together," Tu'ver said.

"Do you find it distracting when you're on duty?" I asked. "If anything, your performance has gotten better.

"You've been rating my performance on duty?" Tu'ver asked.

"I meant that as a good thing and you know it," I shot back. Tu'ver laughed.

"I forget you're not as cowed by me as much as the others are. Takes the fun out of it," he shrugged.

"I still know enough to know that, if it came down to it, you'd kill me with no regrets," I assured him.

"You're wrong. I'd feel bad for a bit," Tu'ver corrected.

I laughed. He was joking. Right?

"Besides, I could only kill you if I snuck up on you. You'd win in hand-to-hand."

"You're right about that," I agreed. "But I didn't seek you out to talk about the ways we could kill each other."

"But that's so much fun," Tu'ver grinned. "To answer your question, if anything, Mariella helps me do better in the field. She goes out of her way to make sure things are nice and comfortable in our quarters when I get back. I strive to be worthy of the consideration she gives me."

"I'm not sure how much of a homemaker Amira is." The mental image of her tidying up our cabin and waiting for me to come home was laughable. "Knowing her, she'll probably fight to be in the thick of things more often than not."

"That's one thing I'm grateful for," Tu'ver shook his head. "Mariella has no desire to be in the thick of things. Unless it's something like this, I don't expect to see Mariella in the heat of battle any time soon."

"Amira proved to be surprisingly well suited to the

heat of battle," I continued. "Did you see her shooting when the Xathi attacked the *Vengeance*? I think I fell in love with her right then and there."

"I didn't see that, unfortunately," Tu'ver replied. "But it's not hard to believe. Amira is definitely spirited."

"Yes, she is." I was proud, I couldn't help it.

"So, when are you going to tell her?" Tu'ver asked.

"I have no idea," I confessed. "I want to tell her right now, but if she rejects me, that'll make the rest of this excursion quite awkward."

"Do you think she would reject you?"

"Honestly?" I glanced at Tu'ver. "No. Obviously, we're attracted to each other physically but it's more than that. I genuinely believe she cares about me."

"So, what's stopping you?" Tu'ver asked.

"I don't want to be a distraction," I explained. "All of us need to be focused on getting through this labyrinth and securing whatever is waiting for us at the center. We've already encountered enough hazards as it is."

"I suppose that's reasonable," Tu'ver shrugged.

"How did you tell Mariella?" I asked.

"I didn't make an official declaration to announce how I felt," Tu'ver explained. "It just sort of…happened. We started out as friends but even then, there was always something more between us."

"So, I should be Amira's friend for now and wait to see what happens?" I clarified. Tu'ver just laughed.

"If there's anything you need to know about human women, it's this: they all have a different mating ritual. What Mariella likes is probably not what Amira likes. You've got to figure it out for yourself," Tu'ver said.

"That sounds like a headache," I sighed.

My mind wandered to Leena and Axtin. Out of all the human females I've encountered, Leena was the most like a Valorni. No wonder Axtin took to her right away.

"If you're meant to be with Amira, the things you do will naturally attract her to you," Tu'ver continued. "If you continue to be exactly who you are, she'll come to you if she likes it. Which, considering how nice she's been lately, I think she does."

"You make it sound so simple, yet so complicated at the same time." I shook my head.

"Welcome to the world of human females." Tu'ver grinned as we continued our slow walk and came within earshot again. "There's nothing like them in any galaxy."

"I heard that!" Mariella called from a few paces ahead of us.

"It was a compliment, my love," Tu'ver replied.

Their voices had drawn Amira's attention. Her gaze found mine. I winked. She grinned back.

That was a good thing, right?

AMIRA

"There's so little to study, I can't help but feel disappointed," I admitted to Zan. He might be a pain in the ass, but he was my closest connection to the Aeryx.

If I wanted to understand anything about them, about why they built this place, I'd have to make nice.

"Understandable." He spoke without looking up from the map. "As I understand it, you humans are lacking anything of note in the archeological department."

"Only on this planet," I said dryly. "On Earth, there were hundreds of ancient cultures just waiting to be dug up."

"Does that do any good now?" Zan asked.

"Not as much as I thought it would," I answered

honestly. "I'm feeling quite unprepared for all of this." It was okay for my pride to take this hit if it paid off in the end.

At least, that's what I told myself.

"Again, understandable."

My smile tightened at the corners of my mouth. "Fen sang your praises back on the *Aurora*," I pressed. "She said you an expert in the races the Xathi were keen on. Is that true?"

Now I had his attention. He looked up from the map and fixed me in his unusual gaze.

"She said that?"

I could tell he was pleased with the thought.

"She did," I confirmed. "And now it appears you're my only hope if I'm to understand any of this." I gestured to the space around us.

"I'll try to be of assistance."

"Who were the Aeryx?" I asked. "How can they have left so little behind?"

"That is not so simple of a question," Zan began. "Fen may call me an expert, but the reality of it is that the Aeryx always leave behind little. The details of who they were are quite sparse."

"You must know something," I pleaded.

"They were masters of space travel. We know that to be true. And we are fairly sure that they had an extraordinary ability to adapt quickly to a variety of environments," Zan explained.

"And that was due to their advanced technology?" It would've had to be. The Xathi wouldn't be interested in chasing a ghost race otherwise.

"Yes. The single set of Aeryx remains ever found did not display anything that suggested natural abilities to do such."

"What about the others?" I wished I could stop and take notes, but I didn't want to halt our progress. "The races the Xathi were interested in?"

"The Xathi have been known to show interest in the Zantrians and the Lo." Zan recited, as if giving a lecture to a slightly slow student. "The Zantrians have proved to be far easier to learn about. They were masters of genetic coding. They can influence their own genetic makeup and are biologically compatible with many other species. You'd be amazed at how many people have traces of Zantrian in their genetic makeup. You could have it and not even be aware."

"That would be something," I nodded. The moment I got back to the *Aurora*, I was going to have my genetic makeup sequenced.

"Their gene-modifying technology also helped perfect the individual Zantrian. Birth defects, anomalies, even a less favorable eye color could be corrected with their technology. They were quite clever when they built it. When other species try to use Zantrian genetic modifying tech, it is usually a fatal encounter."

"But it wasn't for the Xathi?" I asked.

"No, it was. The Xathi took components of their modification technology and reworked it to their own species."

"And what about the Lo?"'

"The Lo were the most fearsome space warriors ever known. Even your green friend pales in comparison." I snuck a peek over my shoulder at Dax, who was listening to something Mariella was saying.

"Are there any Lo to be studied?" I brought my attention back to Zan.

"Alas, no. The Lo were one of the first races the Xathi overtook. It was the Lo that introduced the Xathi to so many of the tactics they use today."

"How did the Xathi know to target these specific races? Was it simply trial and error?" I asked.

"No," Zan replied. "The Xathi learned about them from us."

"Oh," I said softly. I'd forgotten that the Urai had created the Xathi race by mistake. I spoke quickly, not wanting to make Zan uncomfortable. "Thank you for sharing your knowledge."

"It is not often I get to talk about it. I enjoyed the conversation," Zan admitted.

"Come talk to me about it whenever you want," I offered. "I'll always be interested." I was about to ask about the map when white-hot pain tore through my body. I tried to scream, I tried to jerk away, but I couldn't.

"Amira!" I could hear Dax shouting for me, but I couldn't answer.

I tried to call out to him, but my whole body felt as if it were made of stone. The pain was so blinding, so intense, I wanted to pass out. I didn't know how I was still standing.

You're okay, I coached myself. *Just breathe.* But I couldn't. I tried to take air into my lungs, but nothing was happening. My body wasn't responding.

"They're paralyzed!" I heard Mariella yell.

I turned the word over in my mind, grateful to focus on something other than the pain. That couldn't be right. Didn't that come from getting hit, or an accident, or... Oh, god I needed to breathe.

"Don't get too close," Tu'ver warned.

Dax must have tried to reach me. I wished I could see him. All I could see was the endless black hallway ribboned with bands of light. Zan stood out of the corner of my vision, but I couldn't move my eye to look at him more clearly. Was he okay?

"We've got to do something, now!" Dax shouted. "Look for something to switch it off."

My vision was going blurry. My lungs burned as they begged for air that wouldn't come. The panic spinning inside me suddenly evaporated and I thought, with uncanny clarity, of Jeneva.

She'd be devastated if Dax, Tu'ver, and Mariella returned without me.

I'm so sorry, Jeneva. I should've been better.

"Up there!" Tu'ver shouted. "It looks like some sort of generator."

I didn't dare let myself feel relief. Not yet. My vision was going dark. I would lose consciousness soon.

I heard the mechanical clicking of Dax's crossbow as he loaded a bolt. A moment later, I heard a whoosh as it soared somewhere overhead, followed by a thunk and a crackle as it hit its target. The stinging pressure surrounding me lessened. I was able to suck in the smallest breaths of air. I had to do this carefully. If I fell unconscious, I don't think I'd survive. I just needed to hold on until Dax broke the generator.

"It's creating a force field!" I heard him yell. There was another whoosh of a bolt. But instead of hearing it meet its target, I watched it bounce off something above me and clatter to the floor.

I took another small gulp of air and held it in my lungs for as long as I could. Small, controlled gulps every few seconds followed by slow, careful exhales. I toed the line somewhere between consciousness and unconsciousness.

"I can't get through it," Dax cried out. "I'm going to go in to get them."

"Dax, no!" Mariella shouted.

I would've said the same thing. I could barely breathe, there was no way he'd be able to walk through the field to get me and Zan. I could hear Mariella crying softly and Tu'ver murmuring consolations.

Dax must've gotten stuck.

Oh, Void. Not Dax. He had to be alright.

Something slowly wrapped around my wrist. A palm against my skin, then, one by one, fingers closing around my arm.

Dax.

He pulled on my arm. At first, I wouldn't budge, but Dax was relentless. Eventually, I began to move. It was like I was being dragged through almost dry cement. As Dax pulled me, I continued to focus on my breathing. I had to stay awake.

After what felt like hours, the pressure around me burst like a bubble and I collapsed on the stone floor.

"Oh my God, Amira!" Mariella sobbed. She pulled me against her, tilting me up so I could see and breathe better.

"Dax," I croaked. My throat felt like it'd been electrocuted.

"He went back for Zan," Tu'ver explained. My vision came back to me in pieces. First, I was able to distinguish the black stone from the pale bands of light. Then I could make out the shapes of Tu'ver and Mariella hovering over me.

I lifted my head to look towards the energy field I'd been pulled from. Dax was in the thick of it, slowly moving closer to Zan.

"He shouldn't have…" I said weakly. I was all I could manage.

"Don't try to talk yet," Tu'ver instructed. "Just try to stay still."

Dax had reached Zan. Zan had been in there so much longer, I hoped he was okay. Dax started moving backward. It took him nearly ten minutes to escape the field. When he was out, both he and Zan fell to the floor.

"Dax," I called out, hot tears burning my eyes.

He panted and coughed as he crawled across the floor to reach me. Tu'ver went to see to Zan and Mariella gently shifted me so that I was lying on Dax's chest for support.

"You'll be okay," Dax soothed. "You're going to be just fine."

"Zan's alive!" Tu'ver called to us.

"Thank you," I rasped.

Dax was on his feet before both me and Zan. Dax

helped me sit up until I could do it on my own. He helped me drink water as soon as I was able to. Standing and walking were more of a challenge. Zan recovered first, as wobbly as a newborn Luurizi for a few minutes.

My equilibrium was totally thrown out of sorts. The room tipped and hitched around me as I tried to keep my balance. Dax kept a firm hand on my back until I could stand on my own. The moment I could walk without any help from a person or a wall, Dax looked at me and folded his arms across his chest.

"We're leaving," he commanded.

DAXION

"You can't be serious!"

Color rose in Amira's cheeks. I knew that gleam in her eye. She was going to fight me on this.

I wasn't so foolish as to expect otherwise.

"Do you think I would joke about this?" I asked her. "Amira, you and Zan almost died!"

"I know that," she shot back. "But we didn't!"

"Only because we were there to save you," I said, nodding to Tu'ver and Mariella.

"That's why we work in teams, isn't it?" she pleaded desperately. "When you or Tu'ver or Mariella end up in danger, I'll be there to help you."

I sighed and pressed my fingers into the bridge of my nose. I knew arguing was useless.

These ruins meant so much to Amira. She wouldn't walk away from them without a good fight.

But couldn't she see the danger she was in? The danger we were all in?

I'd never felt fear the way I did when I saw she was trapped in that energy field. I didn't think I was going to be able to pull her out.

Being in that field put an immense strain on my body. She was delicate, easily harmed. I could only imagine what it had done to hers.

"This is simply too risky, Amira," I tried again. "The moment we got here, we fell through a trapdoor. We've climbed up walls as the floor crumbled beneath us. I was attacked by some kind of stone creature. Now you and Zan nearly died in some sort of paralysis-inducing energy field. It's not just that this place is dangerous, it's that we can't even begin to understand exactly how dangerous!"

"But we've come so far," she begged. "No one else has even set foot in here before. None of my people knew this existed. How can any of you even think of turning your back on it?"

"What good can we do if we die down here?" Mariella asked, gently.

I shot her a grateful look.

"You, of all people, should be on my side!" Amira turned her piercing gaze to Mariella.

"This isn't about sides. It's about survival," I interjected. "Our chances of survival are far too low to justify this little expedition."

I should've chosen my words more carefully. I could see it in Amira's eyes that I'd offended her.

"This *little expedition* could turn the tides of the Xathi war!" she exclaimed. "We aren't just bumbling around in old ruins for the sake of adventure. We're in Aeryx ruins, a race known to be targeted by the Xathi."

"That doesn't mean there's anything here for us," I said as gently as I could manage. "Perhaps the Xathi have already picked their way through here."

"You *know* that's not true." Amira squared her shoulders.

"No, I don't know that. None of us do. All we have to go on are theories," I argued.

"Theories that have withstood a variety of tests for thousands of years," Zan jumped in.

"See!" Amira exclaimed, her eyes brightening. "Thank you, Zan."

"Do not thank me. I believe we should leave, as well," he corrected.

"But the power signature showing up on your scanners. It *has* to be something!" she cried.

I admired her relentlessness, I truly did, but I wasn't going to let this go, either. I'd prefer it if she would agree to leave, but I wasn't above carrying her out if I had to.

Nothing was worth risking her safety.

"Yes, there are power signatures, but we don't know what's causing them," Zan explained.

"We can make an educated guess," Amira argued.

"It depends on your definition of educated," Zan replied.

Amira rolled her eyes.

"I'm willing to bet it has something to do with space travel." Amira gave a decisive nod of her head. "That's what the Aeryx specialize in, isn't it?"

Zan hesitated a moment before touching his speech pad. "Yes."

"So, it wouldn't be too much of a leap to assume that they're keeping something down here that could help the Xathi travel through space more efficiently," Amira continued.

"A leap is a leap," I said.

"What if we leave now and the Xathi find this place?" Amira asked. "What if there is something down here that can help them get off this planet? What if they get a hold of something that helps them move to other worlds? It would be our fault for not stopping it when we had the chance!"

"And what if we press on, lose one or two team

members on the way down, only to find something highly radioactive or an unstable thermocore?"

"The Aeryx didn't use thermocores. Their technology exceeds..."

"Not the time, Zan," I huffed.

"Apologies," Zan replied.

"We are on the verge of an extraordinary discovery!" Amira cried out.

"Amira, enough!" I said sharply.

Her mouth closed, and she glared at me with narrowed eyes.

"Look, you're right. There's a chance that there's something important in the center of the ruins. There's a chance the Xathi are after it. But it's not a big enough chance for the rest of us to risk our lives going after it."

"He's right, Amira," Mariella said gently.

Tu'ver only nodded.

She looked at all of us for a long while, then her shoulders sagged.

"Okay." She raised her hands in surrender. "I can't force you to risk your lives for this. If everyone thinks that leaving is the smartest idea, then I'll go."

"I'm glad you're seeing reason," I said, offering my hand to her, but she didn't take it.

"I need a moment alone." She gave me a blank look.

There was no anger or sorrow in her eyes, just

defeat. I would've preferred anger, but I knew I'd hurt her.

"All right," I conceded. "If you want to talk, I'm here."

She nodded. I was dismissed.

I walked over to where Tu'ver and Zan were consulting over the maps.

"We can't go back this way," Tu'ver said. "That corridor collapsed. Why doesn't your map reflect the change?"

"Perhaps your enhancements improperly calibrated it," Zan replied.

"Not that again," I snapped.

Tu'ver and Zan fell quiet.

"Zan, I don't care how. Just find us the safest way out of here."

"Right away." Zan walked off to conduct more scans.

I looked down the corridor at Amira, sitting with her back pressed against the wall and a thoughtful expression on her face.

"You're making the right call." Tu'ver gave me a brotherly clap on the shoulder.

"I know I am," I sighed. "But Amira doesn't see that yet. All she sees right now is that I'm taking her dream away."

"She'll thank you when she lives a long happy life," Tu'ver replied. "And nothing says we can't come back later, better prepared."

"I should go talk to her, away from everyone else. I think that was my mistake," I admitted. "I should've spoken to her privately first."

"I don't think the outcome would've been any different," Tu'ver shrugged. "If it helps, she hates all of us right now, not just you."

"Is that supposed to make me feel better?" I asked.

"Did it?"

"No."

"Then no, it wasn't." I knew Tu'ver was trying.

This wasn't his forte any more than shooting a sniper rifle was mine.

"In all seriousness, give her some time."

"Does that work with you and Mariella?" I asked.

"I don't know. I've never shattered Mariella's dreams before."

I saw the smile tugging at the corner of Tu'ver's mouth.

"Do you want to know what the wall tastes like? I'd be happy to show you."

I couldn't help but laugh, too. Mariella strode over, our pitiful laughter catching her attention.

"That was rough," she winced.

"Yes, it was. Tu'ver was just giving me some incredibly useless advice," I replied.

"You did the right thing." Mariella gave my arm a gentle squeeze.

"Thank you. I hope you're right." I risked another glance at Amira.

"That's exactly what I told you, and you threatened to smash my face into the wall," Tu'ver said incredulously.

"Yes, but Mariella's nicer," I replied.

"Ha!" Mariella stuck her tongue out at Tu'ver, who looked at her like she was the most valuable thing under the sun.

"Did Tu'ver also tell you to give her space?"

"Yes, but I don't like that idea any better coming from you," I replied. "Amira doesn't trust easily. I feel like I've just broken anything we might have started building between us."

"She might feel that way now," Mariella allowed. "But she's not stupid. She'll see reason if we just let her be for a while. If I was in her shoes, I'd be upset, too."

"I need her to understand that I'm only doing this to keep her safe," I stressed.

"She will," Mariella repeated. "If she's anything like her sister, you need to let her come to you."

"Good news, everyone!" Zan chimed in. "I have recalibrated my devices."

He threw a look in Tu'ver's direction.

Tu'ver narrowed his eyes, daring the Urai to continue carefully.

"I have been able to detect the most structurally

sound way out of here. It is a bit of a walk, but we can be almost certain that nothing will come crashing down on us."

"Sounds just like what we're looking for," I nodded. "But on the off chance there's a cave-in, I'll go first."

"You will not hear an argument from me," Zan replied as he double checked his packs.

"I'll get Amira," Mariella offered.

I nodded my thanks.

She'd come around.

She'd understand.

She had to, right?

AMIRA

My head ached from conflicting thoughts, racing against each other like a pair of battling aramirions.

I had to get to the center of this place, there was no doubt in my mind about that.

Whatever created that massive power signature was important. I wasn't leaving without it.

There wasn't room for debate, whatever Dax or any of the others might think.

Zan could dismiss it all as an overly optimistic theory, but I knew in my gut that I was right.

I couldn't bear to take another step, knowing that eventually the Xathi would find this place.

I couldn't live with myself knowing that I'd had the

chance to prevent more death and destruction and didn't take it.

For once in my life, I was a help instead of a hindrance.

I just needed a chance to make my escape...

But I wasn't so naïve as to think my actions wouldn't have consequences.

The others would be angry when they realized I'd gone back into the depths of the ruins.

They'd think me selfish, desperate to fulfill my archeological dreams.

I hoped by now they'd realize there was more to me than that, but my track record didn't really speak highly of me.

There was a chance that they would come after me. More than a chance, really. I could almost guarantee they would try to track me down.

I debated telling them that I was going to go back. Surely they'd try to stop me, but at least I could tell them not to follow me.

I opened my mouth to call out to them, but quickly stopped myself.

Who was I kidding? Telling them was a stupid idea.

I was sure I couldn't be convinced not to go back for whatever was hidden in this temple, but if Dax decided to throw me over his shoulder and force me out, there wasn't much I'd be able to do about that.

I was confident in Dax's desire to protect me.

He wouldn't feel the least bit guilty about dragging me out of here against my will if he thought it was the only way to keep me safe.

Maybe getting close to him was a mistake.

If I didn't care about him, it wouldn't be so difficult to deceive him like this.

I retracted the thought as soon as I formed it. I could never regret growing close to Dax.

But where we truly as close as I thought we were?

It happened all the time.

Two people who are attracted to each other get thrown into a high risk, high adrenaline situation and form a close bond. Then when they go back to the real world, their regular routine and responsibilities, that bond just fizzled away.

What if I was just his adrenaline rush?

Stop that, I scolded myself.

Lying to myself wouldn't lessen my guilt over what I was planning to do.

Dax cared for me.

Sneaking back without his knowledge and against his wishes would hurt him. That was a consequence I'd have to accept.

Perhaps I could get Mariella's attention.

After the last few days I'd come to consider her as a friend. I could tell her where I was going and ask her to keep it quiet until the others noticed. Then, she could tell them I didn't want to be followed.

I sighed.

Not really.

Mariella's priority would be everyone's safety, including mine. She'd never let me sneak off.

She must have noticed I was staring at her. She met my gaze, offered me a kind smile and hung back from the group until I'd caught up with her.

"I know it's frustrating," she said, linking her arm through mine. "I had to give up on a few finds back when I was working as an archivist."

"This is my first and only find," I replied. "Turning my back on it feels like I'm turning my back on myself. More importantly, on everyone we could potentially save with whatever's at the center."

"We'll find another way to help people. There's always another way."

She sounded so sure of it, I almost believed her.

"Not if the Xathi find this place after we leave," I countered.

"We all want to stop the Xathi as much as you do." Mariella's voice was gentle, but I detected a hint of reproach. "It's devastating for all of us to have to turn back when we've come so far."

"I know," I said softly.

Of course, they were all upset.

I wasn't the only one who'd worked hard for this.

"Is there another reason why turning back is so hard for you?" Mariella asked.

"The safety of the planet isn't reason enough?" I chuckled.

Mariella offered a smile.

"It is. But when we were discussing it before, you seemed to take the decision personally," Mariella commented.

She was more observant than I'd given her credit for.

"It's just that," I started, but I hesitated.

Talking about myself like this wasn't one of my strong suits.

"It's just that this is the first time in my life that I've felt useful." I felt embarrassed the moment the words were out of my mouth.

"I'm sure that's not true," Mariella said brightly.

"It is," I insisted. "My parents couldn't understand why I wanted to study archeology. For a long time, I was convinced I'd made the wrong choice, because there's no work for an archaeologist on this planet yet. When Jeneva first went on the *Vengeance*, she was immediately helpful, even if she didn't like anyone. If anything, I feel like I've been unhelpful in every way. This was my chance to change that, and now I'm walking away from it."

"I think you're being too hard on yourself," Mariella said. "I grew up in Leena's shadow. I know what it's like to feel like the less valuable sibling. It took me forever to realize I was useful even if I wasn't doing as much as Leena was."

"You cured a disease, Mariella," I reminded her.

"Technically, that was Leena," she corrected.

"But you made it possible. You didn't have to turn back on your chance to prove yourself."

This little chat wasn't making me feel any better. If anything, it only made me more determined to go back into the temple.

"Once we get back to the *Aurora*, I think you'll find that no one thinks you're useless," she went on. "Even if you don't return with some magical artifact that will save the day, the entire crew knows you tried. You put your life on the line for their cause. That won't go unnoticed."

"Thanks."

Though it didn't sound like it, I meant it. I knew she was right, but I was convinced that I could do better.

"I think I'd like to walk on my own for a little while longer, if you don't mind."

"Of course." Mariella retracted her arm.

She gave my shoulder a light squeeze before hurrying to the front of the group where Tu'ver and

Dax walked. Dax said something to her and looked over his shoulder at me.

"She just needs a little space," I heard Mariella tell him.

He offered me a sweet smile that sent my heart fluttering before facing forward once more.

Once I was sure he wasn't going to look back again, I slowed my pace.

I knew it was silly to think this way, but I'd started to consider the temple as a sentient entity.

Everything that happened was too strange, too precisely targeted to us to be chance.

I walked closer to the wall, running my hand along one of the colored bands.

I could count on one hand the number of times I'd taken a leap of faith. At least two of those instances involved Dax.

I was prepared to take another.

"Help me get to the center of the temple," I whispered to the glowing band.

I immediately felt stupid. I was talking to a rock. Though, at this point, what could I lose?

Worst case scenario was that nothing changed.

Just as I was thankful I'd only made a fool of myself in my own mind, the faintest of vibrations thrummed through the glowing band. I slowed my pace and tried to look as sulky as possible in case anyone looked back at me.

Maybe my reputation wasn't entirely useless.

I kept my movement to a minimum as I tried to figure out whether or not I really felt something in the wall.

Sure enough, I did. As I walked, the vibrations felt stronger and stronger. I wondered if the bands had been vibrating this whole time, and none of us had noticed it. It was so faint, and I hardly recalled seeing anyone in the party touch the bands for an extended period.

The tips of my fingers tingled as the sensation grew stronger. Right when I thought I'd have to pull my hand away, a gap in the wall revealed itself.

I'd found another illusion passage. I was certain this was my way into the center of the labyrinth.

I risked a glance at the others.

Dax led the way, covering the ground in long strides. Mariella and Tu'ver followed close behind him, chatting amiably. Zan had his face buried in one of his clever gadgets.

It wouldn't take long for them to notice I was missing. I just had to hope they wouldn't find this little passage.

If I had something to leave behind, I would've left

them a note instructing them to stay put until I returned.

If I called out, they'd be sure to follow me, stop me.

I lingered at the mouth of the hidden passageway. A small tug in my chest reminded me that I didn't have to do this. I could run after the others and pretend I never considered going back.

Dax was too large for me to put my arms all the way around him, but I could cling to his arm and not let go until we were back on the *Aurora*. Hell, I bet Dax would carry me out of here if I asked him to.

But I remembered my promise to Jeneva.

I wouldn't run away from the reality of what was happening to my planet. If I didn't do this, I'd just be running away again.

I was going to do my part to end this war or die trying.

I took a deep breath and ducked into the passageway.

DAXION

Thoughts of Amira filled my mind as I walked, scanning for traps despite Zan's reassurances.

She'd trusted me.

How long would it take her to trust me again?

She felt betrayed, I knew it. I just didn't know how to fix anything.

I looked back to check on her, hoping that seeing her might trigger the right words for an apology, but she wasn't there.

I stopped in my tracks.

"What's the matter?" Mariella asked.

"Amira's gone," I answered.

I looked past the others, hoping maybe she had fallen a bit behind, but it was a straight passageway.

She wasn't there.

The others turned around and looked. Tu'ver uttered a soft curse as Zan looked at me.

"Where could she have disappeared to?" he asked of no one in particular.

None of us had an answer.

"We must locate her."

We headed back down the passage. I had no idea where she might have gone, there had been no side passages, no alcoves, nothing.

"Keep your eyes open for any cracks, or holes, or secret passages we might have missed," I said as I ran my hands across the wall.

The others nodded. We spread ourselves out as we searched.

How could I have let her out of my sight?

I should have been at the rear or had Tu'ver at the end of our line. If anything had happened to her, I didn't know how I was going to tell Jeneva.

I didn't know how I was going to live with myself, knowing I had lost her.

My breath came in short, quick bursts. My heart raced, my head pounding with every beat.

I pushed on every inch of wall I could, even punched and kicked some, thinking that if she had fallen into another trap door, it may have closed tightly behind her.

I never kept track of how long we searched, my

mind had been racing through possibilities the entire time. I couldn't think of anything but how I had failed her and what kind of trouble she might have been in.

I imagined all kinds of terrible scenarios. I started to become angry.

In frustration, I punched one of the walls with my full strength and let out a shout.

The others looked at me in sympathy.

Tu'ver walked by behind me.

"We'll find her, brother," he said quietly.

I looked at him, dejected and angry.

"We'll find her," he repeated.

I turned away from him and checked the other side of the passageway, pushing on everything that looked like it might be a trigger for a hidden door. Less than thirty heartbeats passed when Mariella let out a yelp and shouted at us to come over.

She had found something.

We rushed over, and hidden in the shadows of a break in the glowing lines, was a small passageway. It had been easy to miss, almost imperceptible, unless you looked directly at it.

"This has to be it, right?" Mariella said.

She was excited. She had found, we hoped, where Amira had run away from us.

"Let's hope so," I said, still catching my breath.

"Well?" Mariella looked up at me with impatience.

"Are we going or standing here?"

Tu'ver shook his head.

"No. You know as well I as do, we have to return to the *Aurora*, report this."

Mariella spun to him, face pale. "What do you mean? We're not leaving her here!"

My chest tightened, constricted as if I were still in the damn force field. Tu'ver was right. I knew exactly with Vrehx would say about this. Certainly, what General Rhour would think.

The ship, my brothers - that was my family now. My world.

Still, there was no choice.

"Yes, you are," I confirmed as her jaw clenched, lips compressed to a tight line. "You're all returning to the shuttle now. But I'm not."

"We'll come with you. What if there are other traps, or creatures down there?"

Zan's robotic speaker echoed slightly in the thin passageway. "I would prefer to be in the shuttle myself. I have decided field work is not my specialty. I am much more effective in a laboratory and work-room."

"Tu'ver will get all of you out safely." He'd never let anything happen to her.

Just like I couldn't abandon Amira.

"We'll be back as soon as possible."

Tu'ver only nodded in reply, the hardness in his eyes

my confirmation. If something threatened the shuttle, or if they were recalled to the *Aurora*, they'd have to leave us here.

No more time for chatting.

"We'll see you both soon," Mariella insisted.

I hoped so.

With a clone of Zan's map, I turned down the passageway and started my search for Amira.

The passageway was rather tight, there were several times I had to turn sideways in order to pass. As I searched, I thought about my asinine words, actions, and thoughts since this entire mission had started.

I had placed so much attention onto Amira that when I angered her, my mind shut down, and I became oblivious to everything that I was supposed to notice.

If I had been doing my job properly, I would have organized our line better, so that either Tu'ver or myself would have kept a better eye on Amira.

If I was honest with myself, it was my feelings for her that had impaired my judgment during this entire fiasco.

I had been so concerned with her safety that I had decided that the mission was too risky just because of a few traps.

If this mission had been comprised of strike team members, we would have continued on with little hesitation.

We would have discussed the possibilities, then decided that whatever was in the center of this trap-infested labyrinth was worth trying for.

We would have continued the mission until it truly was too dangerous to continue. I would have worried for my team members, as I always did, but we would have gone on.

Whatever this device, or power, or weapon, or... whatever...was hiding in these ruins was, it was worth trying for. It had to be kept out of Xathi hands, even if we couldn't use it ourselves.

Amira had been right the entire time. We had to know what was in here, and I had tried to take her away from it.

She was right not to trust me.

After squeezing through twists and turns, debris began to litter the floor, bathed in the dim light from the strange glowing lines on the walls.

There was something wrong with this passage. I could swear the colors changed when I looked back where I had come, but then I would blink to clear my eyes, and everything looked the same.

I checked the map, not seeing my current route on it. Something was wrong, I'd been traveling too long. Something wasn't right about this part of the ruins, or at least this part of my map.

I was lost, mentally and literally. I had no idea if I

should keep moving forward or turn around. Perhaps I should have brought the others with me.

When the passageway widened into what I thought of as a small room, I stopped. Debris was strewn everywhere, and the hall continued on to my left.

I checked the walls for secret doors, checked the floors for traps, even looked up to see if the ceiling held any surprises. There was nothing except the holes in the ceiling where the rocks had fallen, and those lines of color that were driving me mad.

I had risked the mission, my friends, and a stranger that was willing to help because of my feelings for Amira.

I didn't regret those feelings, I just regretted how those feelings had made me act.

With a scream of frustration, I slammed my fist into the wall.

It didn't change anything.

And I didn't feel a bit better.

I had never thought that I could ever be frustrated so much.

I had fought in battles, nearly died, and been forced to kill.

None of that had frustrated me as much as this woman did.

And like an idiot, I found myself smiling at the idea.

I started my search again.

AMIRA

I used to relish spending time alone. As soon as I was thrown into a situation that demanded I worked with others, I'd hurry through it and make my escape.

Now, as I wandered the glowing halls of the temple, loneliness crept through me and wrapped cold fingers around my heart.

Each time I saw a pretty pattern in the glowing bands, I wanted to point it out to Mariella. I was certain there was more Zan could tell me about the temple. Tu'ver was much nicer than I'd assumed he was.

And I missed everything about Dax.

I was fairly sure I was walking in the right direction, but the crushing silence broken only by the sound of my own breathing made me uneasy. On more than one occasion, I was so sure that someone, or something, was watching me that I felt the need to stop and hide somewhere.

I wasn't armed. There was no way I could've snuck a weapon off Tu'ver or Dax without getting caught.

I had a stun gun in my pack that I'd 'forgotten' to return the night Dax caught me trying to sneak off the *Vengeance*. If another one of those stone guardians appeared, I'd be all but defenseless.

Out of the corner of my eye, I thought I saw a flicker. When I turned to look, I saw nothing. Sure enough, when I continued on my way, I saw it again.

I turned faster this time. I caught one of the glowing bands on the wall flickering back to normal.

I walked over to it and placed my hand on the band. My hand fell right through the wall, or at least that's what it looked like.

It was another illusion passage, more cleverly concealed than any of the others I'd seen so far. Even though I was staring at it head-on, I still couldn't decipher exactly where the passage began.

The band on the wall flickered again. With my hands outstretched, I followed it.

The passage turned out to be incredibly narrow, hardly wider than my shoulders. I kept one hand extended out in front of me and one on the flickering mineral band.

As I moved farther down the passage, I noticed that

the bands grew thicker and greater in number. Now, there was more glowing mineral than there was polished black stone.

Squinting against the building brightness, it was like being inside of an uncut crystal.

I nearly smacked into the wall when the pathway took a sharp left. It was so narrow that I had to turn to my side to go through. It only now occurred to me that this could be a trap, the flickering band acting as a lure for the curious.

At the moment, I had an inch or two of room on either side of my body, but I was sure the path was gradually getting narrower. I would turn back long before I became wedged between the walls.

I turned another corner, thankful the passage didn't narrow any further. A few yards ahead of me, a section of collapsed wall created a small tower of rubble. I couldn't see over it, but high on the wall on the other side of the pile, the flickering light continued.

Pressing my back flat against the wall for leverage, I managed to awkwardly wiggle up the uneven slope. The rough patches of mineral left scrapes on my palms as I grappled for purchase. The highest peak of the tower left less than a foot gap between it and the ceiling.

With my backside pressed against one wall, and my forearm digging into the rough surface of the other, I kicked against the rubble as hard as I could without dislodging myself.

Eventually, it gave away, and I was able to scramble over it and slide down the other side. The passage was narrower on the other side of the rubble.

So narrow that there was no longer space between myself and the wall, but not so much that I couldn't move.

Up ahead, I could see the end of the passageway. From where I was, it looked like it opened into a larger room. Of course, it could just be another illusion.

I inched forward. Up ahead, the glowing band flickered rapidly. The room ahead, if it was really there, looked completely dark.

I was close now, only a few more feet.

The corridor constricted. It was harder to move forward. The rough parts of the wall tugged at my clothing and hair as if it was trying to pull me backward.

The edge of the wall was within reach. There really was a room at the end of the passage.

I stretched as far as I could.

The very tips of my fingers gripped the edge of the wall. I tried to pull myself closer but, to my horror, I was stuck.

"Shit," I gasped.

I was so close.

I was sure if I wiggled myself backward, I could get out, but I wasn't about to give up.

I jerked my body forward as much as I could, for the first time wishing I'd been given Jeneva's smaller bust.

I heard a faint tearing sound.

I couldn't look down to confirm, but I was sure my clothing had torn on the rough stone.

"Damn it!"

I threw my body forward, again and again, making only the smallest bit of progress.

After a few more attempts, I was sore and breathless, but I'd moved about an inch closer to the end of the passage.

Wrapping the tips of my fingers around the edge of the wall, I took hold, sucked in as much as I could, and pulled with every ounce of strength I could muster.

One.

Two.

Three!

I fell face-first into the open room. There were scrapes along my arms, neck, and face deep enough to draw blood, but I didn't care. I'd made it.

I got to my feet and looked around the room. It was completely black.

No glowing bands, no flickering.

I walked along the walls, feeling for an illusion passage, a secret door, or a hidden hatch. Nothing.

My shoulders sagged in disappointment. I'd gone through all of that for nothing.

I walked back to the mouth of the narrow passage. Getting back through it was going to be a bitch, but at least I knew it was possible.

I turned my body sideways once more and was about to step between the walls when the sound of stone grating on stone froze me in my tracks.

On the wall opposite me, a perfectly square door opened. The chamber on the other side was somehow even darker than the one I was in.

I walked through without hesitation, but wasn't more than two steps in when the door slid shut behind me.

"Damn it." I cursed myself for my stupidity.

Panic rose in me as I realized I'd likely just walked right into a trap. I clawed at the door, looking for a way to get it open.

Suddenly, bright white light flooded the room. I blinked, forcing my eyes to adjust. A swirling ball that looked like it was made of vapor floated in the center of the room.

Underneath it was a rectangular pedestal of black stone. I approached it cautiously. When I reached out to touch it, my hand passed right through it.

I felt nothing. Upon closer inspection, I could see some kind of light generator within the pedestal.

"A hologram?" I wondered out loud.

"Correct."

I sprang away from the ball of light.

"What the hell?" I gasped.

"Apologies," a computer-generated voice came from the ball.

"What are you?" I asked, still in shock.

"I am a guardian," it replied. "You activated me the moment you and your party entered this place."

"Could you see us this entire time?" It would explain why I always felt eyes on the back of my neck.

"In a sense," it answered. "I have been monitoring and analyzing your actions since your arrival."

"Why?" I demanded.

"I wanted to know how you found this place and why you came here," it said. "You are the first to enter in over a millennium."

"Did the Aeryx program you?" I stepped closer.

"Yes," it said.

So, it was an AI, after all.

"Do you understand why my team and I have come here?"

"You wish to locate the Gateway and keep it out of the reach of the Xathi."

The Gateway? It had to be what was giving off that power signature.

"That's right," I replied. "Can you help me do that?"

"I am not programmed to make such a choice," it explained. "I am programmed only to monitor and analyze."

"Do you understand what the Xathi are?"

"I do. They have slaughtered so many of my creators."

If I didn't know better, I could've sworn I heard sorrow in the AI's voice.

"The Aeryx wanted to keep the Gateway from the Xathi."

"Then help me," I pleaded.

The AI was silent. I persisted.

"It won't be long until the Xathi finds this place. If they get their hands on the Gateway, thousands of my people will die. Do you want what happened to your creators to happen to my people?"

"The data I have collected indicates that you do not wish to do harm," it spoke. "I will show you how to find the Gateway."

"What does the Gateway do?" I asked.

"It is how my creators traveled through space," the AI replied. "It is heavily guarded, but there are ways to circumnavigate the defenses."

There was a clicking noise, and a small holo-screen popped out of a hidden port in the pedestal. On it was a detailed map of the ruins. One of the many pathways to the center was highlighted.

"The map shows the path the creators used," the AI explained.

"What will I do once I find the Gateway?" I asked.

The AI did not respond.

Instead, it emitted a brilliant flash of light. I took several steps back, startled, pain blooming through my head. It was everything I could do not to stumble and fall on my back as I was momentarily blinded.

It stopped, and I sagged with relief. Within seconds, I was able to see again.

"I have implanted in you the sight necessary to operate the Gateway once you discover it," the AI responded. "This was the most efficient option."

I bit my tongue.

"Thank you." I carefully tucked the screen into one of my side pockets, the headache already subsiding.

I didn't know what else to say. So many questions raced through my mind, they tangled before I could get any out.

But it was too late.

"Protect it from the Xathi."

The AI projection deactivated and I was left in darkness again, but only for a moment.

A new door opened. It looked like it emptied into one of the main corridors.

It was time to find the Gateway.

And see what it could do.

DAXION

"Impossible!" I roared in frustration as I reached a dead end.

There was no sign of Amira, but she couldn't have gone any other way. This wasn't the first dead end I'd come to.

After going through the passage she must have used to break away from the group, I thought I'd find her easily.

I found a second hidden passage shortly after going through the first, but it was too narrow for me to pass through. I doubted Amira took that passage, anyway. The risk of getting wedged was too great.

I checked the walls for more secret passageways, but I couldn't find any.

"Amira!" I yelled out, but it was no use. This place swallowed sound.

"Skrell!" I kicked out, striking the wall.

Chunks of glowing mineral broke loose.

I paced back and forth, trying to get myself under control. Losing my temper would not help me find her any faster.

I was not giving up on her. I would stay in this wretched place until I found her.

After a few long, deep breaths, I was able to think more clearly. The only thing I could do was retrace my steps and make sure I hadn't missed anything.

I was halfway down the corridor when the unmistakable sound of stone grinding against stone shattered the silence behind me.

Amira stepped out from a doorway that, only a moment ago, had been a solid wall. She looked around as if trying to get her bearings before she spotted me.

"Dax!" she cried out.

The most breathtaking smile spread across her face.

She rushed towards me and I closed the distance between us in two large steps.

She threw her arms around my neck. I wrapped my arms around the small of her back, lifting her off the ground to hold her close. To my surprise, she locked her legs around my waist, enveloping me in a full-body hug.

"What were you thinking?" I demanded, clutching her close to me. The icy claw of terror that had gripped my spine ever since she'd left loosened.

"I couldn't just walk away from this place." Her voice was muffled against the fabric of my shirt.

"I know," I sighed and ran a hand along the back of her head. "It was stupid of me to try to make you leave. I should've known I couldn't hold you back."

She pulled back far enough to look me in the eye, a smirk tugging at the corner of her mouth.

"Yes, you should've known," she said.

I rolled my eyes and pulled her in close again, burying my face in the gentle curve of her neck, her unique scent filling my lungs. Now that she was here, in my arms, safe, my heart beat again.

"It was stupid of me to run off without telling anyone, though," she admitted in a small voice. "I won't do anything like that again."

"You better not," I said. "You have no idea what I went through when I realized you'd vanished."

"Really?" She looked up at me again, gnawing her lower lip.

"I didn't realize..." she trailed off.

"That I care for you that much?" I filled in.

"What?" Her head shot up again, almost knocking into my nose.

The mix of shock and delight on her face was incredible.

"It's true, Amira," I repeated. "If I have to, I'll follow you to the ends of the universe." I took another breath of her heady scent, letting it stir me and ease the words. "And that includes the depths of this temple."

"What are you saying?" she asked, her eyes looking at me with nervous excitement.

I paused.

I looked at the creature who had in such a short time changed my entire life.

She had given me cause to fight harder than I hdd before. But more importantly, she would give me a reason to come home after the fight.

My mate. My life.

All my reasons to keep silent fell away, lost in the realization that at any moment she could be lost to me.

"I love you, Amira," I said to her simply.

Now it was her turn to pause.

My heart skipped a beat as her eyes glistened.

If she wasn't ready, if she was never ready to hear me, to want me, it didn't matter. My feelings wouldn't change. I'd protect her, care for--

"I love you, too," she said softly.

I'd never heard sweeter words. I kissed her before she could say anything more. Her hands gripped my shirt, pulling me as close as she could.

The world fell away from us. I forgot about the ruins, the mission, and even the Xathi.

By rights, I should have been doubling back with her to get back to the others on the shuttle, instead of plunging ahead with her to fulfill her mission to find the center of this crazy labyrinth.

But I couldn't.

The only thing that existed to me was Amira.

Her touch, her taste, sent fires through my veins, forcing me to hold still as she squirmed in my arms, her delicate folds sliding against my length, separated only by flimsy, stupid fabric.

I groaned against her throat.

"Careful, my heart."

She rocked against me again, legs tight around my waist. "You know it's never a good idea to keep me from what I want," she murmured, the breath of her words hot against my ear. "And I want this. I want you, Dax."

My arousal was instant, urgent. I closed my hands onto her hips, grinding her core against me until her teasing giggles turned to frantic moans to match my own, her gasps puffing against my chest as her arms tightened around my neck.

I had to have her.

I had to be in her, feel her trembling.

And since we didn't have spare clothes, we'd have to

stop.

Shaking with the effort of control, I set her down gently.

She blinked, lost.

"Clothes, my heart."

I pulled my shirt off, all attention on watching her movements, graceful and mesmerizing.

She stood naked before me. I took in every inch of her. The glowing light from the mineral bands bathed her porcelain skin in shades of green, blue, and purple.

I couldn't help but smile. She looked like part of the *Vengeance* crew in this light. I imagined what she would look like as a Valorni.

She'd be lovelier than the other females by far. But I wouldn't change a single thing about her, my pretty little human.

She looked at me expectantly, her eyes flickering down to my uniform pants. Her slender fingers began to slowly undo them. With each second, her movements became more frantic until she had loosened them enough to pull them down.

I kicked off my boots and stepped out of both them and the pants as I lifted her off the ground once more. Her slender legs locked around my waist as I lifted her higher, seating her on one forearm, bringing her luscious breasts to my mouth. One hand freed, I kneaded the soft flesh while I sucked and nipped at the tight bud of the other, then changed my attentions to the first perfect globe. My hand slid down her silken skin, tracing every curve, until I forced it between us and felt her wet heat.

"Dax!" her scream shattered the stillness as my thumb flicked over the nub of flesh I'd found the previous night with my tongue, circling, then dipping into her, repeating the cycle until she trembled, rigid, breaths coming in shallow pants.

Now.

It had to be now.

Quickly I lowered her, but then she shifted her legs one at a time until they were no longer locked around my waist but slung over my forearms.

Oh, my heart.

She'd chosen to place herself in a position that relinquished all control to me. She looked up, her eyes glittering and filled with lust but also something else, something new.

Trust.

I lowered her gently, entering her slowly.

Her tight heat drew me in, demanded more, ripped at my control.

As I buried myself within her, her eyes never left mine, the pink tip of her tongue tracing her lips.

"Are you alright?" I forced out through gritted teeth.

"More," she panted, then clenched around me, shattering what shreds of self-control I had left.

I drove deeper, lifting her to slide off my throbbing cock, then pulling her back to me, grinding into her with every thrust.

At her first moan, I picked up the pace, pounding, lost in my need to possess her.

She looped her arms around my neck to hold herself upright. I could feel her breasts brush against my bare chest with every thrust.

If I pulled her closer, I bet I could feel her heart beating.

She leaned closer yet, frantically kissing every part of me she could reach until she found my lips. I took her bottom lip between my teeth and bit gently, relishing the gasp it elicited. She rocked her hips, urging me to go faster.

Mine, mine, mine.

The phrase echoed in my head each time I thrust into her. She let out a shuddering gasp and let her head fall back.

I watched the waves of pleasure tear through her body as she reached her peak. And as she tightened around me, my own release ripped through me, tearing a roar from my throat.

We clung to each other, panting and spent.

Her whole body trembled with the force of her

climax. I shifted her so both of her legs were swung over one arm and my other arm looped around her back. With careful balance, I lowered myself to the floor and held her against my chest.

I could've stayed like that for hours, but her skin quickly prickled with goosebumps. Another strange human quirk. I'd learned it meant that they were cold.

"Let's get you back into your clothing."

I pulled her up and rubbed my warm hands over her skin before releasing her. She stood up on wobbly legs and grabbed her clothing. She dressed far faster than I did, rubbing her arms impatiently as she waited for me.

Once I was dressed, she huddled next to me.

"Are you just trying to steal my warmth?" I asked.

"Absolutely," was her unabashed response.

I laughed and pulled her back into my embrace, happy for another reason to hold her. It didn't take long for her to stop shivering.

"So, what was in that room?"

"What?" She looked up at me, her eyes gleaming in the pale light.

"You had just left a room when I found you," I prompted. "Did you find anything?"

"Oh! Right." A blush colored her cheeks.

I pressed my lips onto her hot skin as she dug into her pocket. She pulled out what looked like a thin sheet of glass.

When she held it up, the image flickered to life.

It was a map of the ruins.

"I found an AI left behind by the Aeryx," she explained. "It's been watching and listening to us since we got here."

"Watching?" I cocked an eyebrow, thinking of the show we'd just put on for it.

She shrugged, but her cheeks darkened adorably. "I wasn't thinking." She squirmed against me. "And I wouldn't change a thing. Anyway, it knows we're here to stop the Xathi. It gave me this to help us get to what's in the middle, something it called the Gateway. It's what the Aeryx used to travel through space."

"So, it's some kind of battery?" I asked.

"Maybe. Or possibly a generator? I'm not sure. It has to be some kind of power source, though, judging by the signature it left on Zan's equipment."

Amira tugged on her boots and did up the laces.

"I hope we can figure out a way to transport it," I replied.

Her head jerked up. I grinned as I watched a look of understanding come over her face.

"You mean we can go get it?" Her face split into a grin.

"You found the map, and you made it this far," I smiled back. "It seems like a waste if we turned back now."

Though she only had one boot on, Amira leaped to her feet and ran to hug me. I wrapped my arms around her and lifted her off the ground just to hear her laugh.

"Thank you," she murmured against my neck.

"Anything for you."

AMIRA

Dax and I walked hand in hand through the temple.

I hadn't understood how big the ruins truly were until now. The closer we got to the center, the wider the corridors and the higher the ceilings were.

"I think we're going farther underground," Dax commented.

"I'm sure Zan has some fancy contraption that could tell us exactly how far down we are."

"Do you think he'd want to be here with us?" I asked.

"After the paralysis trap, I think he was ready to leave," Dax replied.

I shuddered, remembering how terrifying it was to feel my lungs frozen within my chest.

"Understandable," I agreed. "That's how any normal person should feel."

"So, you admit you're not normal?" Dax teased.

"Freely," I laughed. "I'm fully aware that a normal person wouldn't do the majority of the things I do."

"I don't know if that makes it better or worse," Dax chuckled.

"You're here, too! You don't get to judge my choices." I gave his shoulder a gentle shove.

He nudged me back in return. Even though he'd done it as gently as possible, it was still enough to shift me by a step or two. Dax pulled me in close again and tucked me under his arm.

"Where are we on the map?" he asked.

I pulled it out of my pocket once more and it glowed to life.

The pathway we were meant to follow started in the chamber where I'd encountered the AI. It was detailed, but it didn't reflect our current position.

"If we've followed this perfectly, we aren't far from the center," I said.

I don't know what we would've done if I hadn't had the map. Nearly every turn required us to locate an illusion passage which would've been impossible if we didn't know exactly where to look.

"There should be a passage up ahead on the left. From there, we take a right pretty soon after, then there's a long stretch that should dump us into the center chamber."

I tucked the map into my pocket once more and ran my hand along the wall until it gave way beneath my hand.

The illusion passageway was so small Dax had to duck his head. We continued on for a few paces before I found the second passageway on the right. Luckily for Dax, the corridor was spacious.

"This should take us right to the center chamber," I reaffirmed.

I reached for Dax's hand, pulling him forward.

"Not too fast," he cautioned me. "We don't know what we're walking into."

I slowed my pace, but not by much, pulling against Dax with all of my weight by the time we reached the end of the corridor.

It didn't really do much, but it made me feel better.

I tugged him into the center chamber. The breath left my body in a rush as I looked around in awe.

What was so striking about the structure of the ruins thus far was that every wall was perfectly straight, and every turn was exactly ninety degrees. This room was different, a perfect circle with a high, domed ceiling.

All of the glowing mineral bands snaked up the curve of the dome and met in a brilliant mesh of color at the highest point. Directly below that, in the exact center of the room, sat a cylindrical stone pedestal. A black stone sphere balanced atop the pedestal.

"Amira," Dax nudged me gently.

He stared intently at a different part of the room. I followed his gaze. He was looking at a section of wall that was different from the black stone and glowing mineral bands.

An endless sea of stars dotted with planets and moons; the edges of the image were jagged, as if someone had chipped away at the stone to find this beneath it.

There were more segments like that one around the perimeter of the room, all showing different arrangements of planets, moons, and stars.

Two of them showed a closer view of the surface of two different planets, one pale and snowy, the other lush and green.

A shooting star shot through one of the segments.

Oh.

My stomach flipped.

This wasn't a still image, a painting, a hologram.

"Dax, what are those?" I asked, though deep down, I already knew.

"I think it's a rift," he murmured. "What we're seeing is another part of space."

"Gates," I gasped.

I looked back at the black sphere sitting on the pedestal.

"Dax, I think that's the Gateway. It opens rifts in space. That's how the Aeryx were able to reach so much of the universe."

I strode up to the pedestal and examined the sphere.

As if recalling old memories and thoughts, images flooded my brain.

This was the reason for the blinding white light that the AI had shone in my eyes. Instructions on what to do and how to use it rose in my mind.

Several glowing dots sparkled on the sphere's surface. A white one, slightly larger than the others, and six smaller ones reflecting the same colors I'd seen in the glowing mineral bands. There were six glowing panels in the room.

Six colored dots.

Six rifts.

"I'm certain this is what's controlling the rifts," I explained to Dax. "I'm going to try to close them."

"What?" Dax frowned. "What makes you think you know how?"

"Trust me?"

His face tightened with worry and panic gripped me. If after everything, everything he'd said, everything we'd done, I still hadn't earned his trust…

"Do it."

I nodded, releasing a breath I hadn't realized I was holding. I gingerly touched one of the smaller colored lights on the sphere's surface.

One of the rifts flickered and wavered, but didn't close.

On a hunch, I mimicked the motion I'd move my fingers in to shrink something on a data pad. The rift grew smaller but didn't disappear entirely. I practiced widening and narrowing it with that same motion.

"Amazing," I gasped.

I looked up at the rifts again. Far off in the distance, between the stars, I spied a spaceship lazily drifting through space.

I wondered if whoever was on board could see the rift. Did they know I was watching them?

"Something just occurred to me," Dax said.

"What's that?" I replied, keeping my gaze on the rifts.

"When our weapon malfunctioned, it caused a rift to open. Of course, we had no control over where the rift opened, but now, I'm thinking that the rift opened where it did because this was here," Dax explained. "I've no way to prove that, but it's worth considering."

"I bet you're right." I looked over my shoulder and grinned at him. "In that case, I'd like to thank the Aeryx for building this, for it brought you to me."

"I'm going to try one more thing," I said, mostly to myself.

I placed one fingertip on the white dot and another on a colored dot. The corresponding rift snapped closed. I couldn't help but laugh.

"I did it!" I quickly closed the other rifts.

The last thing I wanted was some other horrible, dangerous alien race falling into my world.

"My mate is brilliant," Dax praised.

Heat flooded my cheeks.

Mate. I liked that.

Brilliant was also nice.

"My mate is pretty great, too," I replied, unable to stop smiling. "Now, let's get the Gateway back to the *Aurora*."

I grasped the sphere and lifted it slowly off the pedestal. The sphere was heavy, but not unbearably so.

I'd be able to carry it out, if I cradled it close to my chest as if it were an infant.

"Do you think you can find your way back from where you found me?" I asked Dax, hugging the sphere against my chest.

"I think so," Dax replied. "I didn't take many turns off the main corridor when I was looking for you. Plus, having a detailed map of the layout will help."

"I hope it won't take very long," I replied. "I hate that we're keeping the others waiting."

"They're probably asleep in the transport unit, infinitely safer than we are," Dax joked.

"You're probably right." I glanced over my shoulder to get a last look at the center chamber.

I paused.

From somewhere in the chamber, there was a grating noise that sounded like a mixture of stone sliding against stone and rocks breaking apart by force.

"Do you hear that?" I looked back to Dax.

He'd stopped, too, only responded with a curt nod.

I looked around the room. Nothing moved or gave any other indication of making any noise, but the sound persisted. It was growing louder.

"Amira, get back!" Dax shouted, pushing me away from the center.

"What?" I stumbled backward until I stood against the wall.

"It's coming from beneath us," Dax said.

I turned my gaze to the stone floor. The rumbling grew louder.

Suddenly, a crack appeared in the floor a few feet to the left of the exact center.

"What the hell?" I gasped as more cracks appeared.

It sounded as if something was being rammed into the floor from below.

A deformed head broke through the surface.

"Is that a hybrid?" I shrieked.

I'd never gotten a good look at one of the hybrids, but even the ones I'd seen from a distance looked nothing like this.

It's head was completely covered in a thick layer of crystal growth to the point where it was impossible to tell where it's a face was. The large spike protruding from its head must have been how it broke through the stone.

It gave another hard thrust upward, shattering more of the stone, enough so that it could get its shoulders and arms free. It shrieked and howled in obvious pain. It had broken many of its own spikes as it clamored up into the chamber.

It couldn't stand upright. It let out one last howl before falling to the floor, still and silent.

"Is it...dead?" I asked, tightening my grip on Dax's arm.

"I think so," Dax replied.

"Should we put it back in the hole?" I wondered.

It didn't seem right to just leave it. It was a person once.

But before Dax could answer, another noise came from the hole, like claws scraping across stone.

Another hybrid sprung from the hole. This one looked more like a person, with only a thin layer of crystal coating its body and no protruding spikes.

Its beady gaze settling on us as I shrank back against the wall, arms tightening around the sphere.

It let out a horrible, high-pitched shriek and, faster than I thought anything could move covered in that hideous crystal, charged.

Dax stepped forward, his fist connecting with the hybrid's skull hard enough to fracture the crystal.

There was a sickening crunch as its neck twisted in the wrong direction. It fell to the floor in a heap.

But it didn't matter.

More bubbled up from the hole in the ground in a mad frenzy, each one widening the gap for the next wave.

Within moments, we were surrounded.

DAXION

I tried to keep Amira between myself and the wall, but it was difficult. The hybrids came at us from all sides. Every time I struck at one, it left her vulnerable for precious seconds.

She grabbed a stun gun from her pack, one of the standard issue ones given to each crew member on the *Vengeance.*

Where the ...

oh.

Despite myself, my lips twisted in an amused smile. Her thievery paid off in the end.

If we got out of this, I'd certainly never be bored.

Not if.

When.

She hit her marks with impressive precision, but the

stun gun only did so much. When it made contact with a hybrid, I don't think it caused them pain, so much as it startled them back a few steps.

However, it gave me time to retrieve my crossbow. My bolts pierced the crystal shell of the hybrids, but I could only shoot at one at a time. Between my bolts and the stun gun, we kept them at bay.

Barely.

There was no organic material I could easily harvest to make more bolts. I considered chipping away at the mineral bands and using the stone chunks, but harvesting them would take time I didn't have.

When I was down to my last bolt, I used it as a close-range weapon, hacking and slashing at the hybrids. The jagged tip cut through some of them as if they were made of clay, for others it sent a shower of crystal shards out in every direction.

I wanted to talk to Amira, to reassure her that everything would be fine, that I would get her out of this.

But she wasn't stupid. She knew as well as I did how dire our situation was becoming.

A hybrid managed to duck around me, lunging for the Gateway.

Amira's stun gun had little effect on it.

I twisted around and grabbed it by the base of the

neck before smashing its head into the wall beside Amira. I wasn't sure if I killed it or knocked it out.

Either way, it wasn't a problem anymore. I shoved its body to the side, hoping to create a bit of a barrier that would slow the others.

"Dax, look out!" Amira cried.

She fired her stun gun again. Yet another hybrid charged, too close behind the first for me to do anything but try to block its blows. I whacked at it with my bolt, but it was almost on top of me.

Its arm was completely encrusted with crystal, formed to make a single spike. The tip of the spike pointed right at my throat. I did my best to hold it back, but the crystal was smooth and hard to grip.

I felt Amira's hand on my back.

I hated that she had to see this.

I'd failed her, in so many ways.

Suddenly, the hybrid's head exploded.

Crystal shards rained down, slicing the exposed skin of my face and arms.

"What the fuck?" Amira rasped behind me, her words echoing my thoughts.

To my left, another hybrid's head burst open. It fell to the floor, dead. It was as if it had been shot…

"Tu'ver's here somewhere," I shouted to Amira.

She let out a relieved laugh. We heard the distinct

sound of firing blasters. Mariella and Zan must be nearby, as well.

I wanted to look for them, but I didn't dare take my eyes off the still encroaching hybrids. They didn't seem dissuaded by the blaster or sniper shots. They were determined to get to the Gateway.

Tu'ver took out hybrids as they crawled up into the room until they stopped coming. Zan and Mariella kept the hybrids from getting too close to Amira. I took them out with my bolt as they slowly made their way closer to me.

Together, we made quick work of them.

The last hybrid standing stumbled towards me.

"Hold fire!" I commanded.

I dove for the hybrid. This one only had a thin layer of crystal coating its skin, so translucent I could still see human features.

I subdued it, pinning it as it writhed to no avail against my iron grip around its neck..

"Amira!" Mariella and Zan stepped out of their hiding place in a corridor opposite the one we'd come through.

Amira ran to hug Mariella.

Tu'ver jumped down from a rocky ledge high above us.

"How did you even get up there?" I laughed.

"Wouldn't you like to know?" Tu'ver replied with a

knowing grin before turning his focus to the remaining hybrid.

"Can you understand me?" he asked in the native tongue of the humans.

The hybrid gave a jerky nod. It must have been indoctrinated recently.

Tu'ver grasped the hybrid's face in his hand, forcing it to look him in the eye.

"Tell me why you came here," Tu'ver demanded.

The hybrid snarled and shrieked.

Tu'ver tightened his grip on the hybrid's jaw. I heard the sound of crystal cracking.

"Tell me," Tu'ver repeated.

"Orders from the queen," the hybrid gurgled, sounding as if even its tongue had turned to crystal.

"How did the queen know?" I asked, pulling its head back into an uncomfortable angle.

It struggled against me but said nothing.

"How did the queen know?" I repeated.

"From the source," it rasped.

"What does that mean?" Tu'ver demanded. "What source?"

The hybrid began to shriek as if someone had struck it with a hot iron. I held its neck at an uncomfortable angle, but it shouldn't have caused it that much pain.

It writhed and shrieked and clawed at itself until I had to release it.

I had my weapon at the ready in case it attacked, but it didn't.

"What's wrong with it?" Amira asked from a few paces behind me.

"I don't know, but keep your distance," I warned her.

The hybrid began to claw at its head. Its screams grew louder and more panicked, until its body suddenly seized up. There was a crunching noise, then it crumpled in a heap on the floor.

"Skrell," Tu'ver snapped. "We need to know how the queen knew to come here."

"Is it...dead?" Mariella's voice was barely above a whisper.

I nodded.

Amira placed a hand on her shoulder to comfort her.

"How did it die?" Zan asked, stepping closer to the body.

"Careful," I warned, but he waved me off.

"Amazing," he said after examining the dead hybrid. "The crystal shell around its head is cracked from the inside."

"The queen must've known it was about to tell us something," Tu'ver reasoned. "She crushed its mind."

"How horrible," Amira sighed.

"It's not like we could have done anything," Tu'ver replied.

"Would you have killed it if we'd gotten the information we needed?" I asked him.

He pondered for a moment.

"I'm not sure," he answered. "It was still so human compared to the others. I don't think it would've sat right with me if I did."

"Me, either," I replied. "It might have made a good test subject for Dr. Parr. She's still trying to solve the mystery of hybridism."

"Would that have been any better for it?" Amira wondered.

"Probably not," I admitted. "Either way, at least it's escaped control of the Xathi queen."

"We should block the way they came in," Tu'ver said after a beat of silence.

"With what?" Mariella asked.

Tu'ver said nothing, only glanced at the fallen hybrids.

"Oh."

"We'll take care of it, don't worry," he assured her with a soft smile.

Tu'ver and I got to work, pushing the fallen hybrids down the tunnel they'd come through. If any more tried to make their way into the temple, hopefully that would dissuade them, but I doubted it would.

Amira surprised me by helping us move the bodies with a grim expression plastered on her face.

"Thank you for coming after us," she said to Tu'ver when the gruesome task was done.

"Once we had mapped the route back to the shuttle, we couldn't just sit there," he replied with a wry smile. "Glad we got here when we did."

"How did you find us?" I asked.

"Funny you should ask," Tu'ver gave me a knowing look. "Zan has a device that can detect changes in temperature. It only worked for us because we happened upon an area the two of you had occupied shortly beforehand. Whatever you were doing generated a lot of heat."

Amira looked away, blushing.

"After that, the heat signatures were fairly easy to follow."

"Lucky for us." I clapped him on the shoulder. "We should leave soon. No doubt the Xathi queen has already deployed another army of hybrids or worse. Amira, do you have that map?"

"What map?" Zan asked with sudden interest.

Amira quickly explained the AI program she'd found.

"We could use the map and go on foot," Amira said, "or we could try to use this."

She held up the sphere.

"What is that?" Mariella wondered.

"It's called a Gateway. It opens rifts between one

point of space and another. It's how the Aeryx traveled long distances," Amira explained.

She turned to Zan. "I figured out how to close rifts, but I don't know how to open them. Do you know anything about this?"

"A broken device like this was found at another Aeryx site. I studied it extensively, though it was not nearly as useful as a working one would've been," Zan explained. "I have some idea of how it might open a rift."

Zan placed a dark blue fingertip on the white dot of light on the sphere's surface. Hair-thin lines of light appeared all over the surface of the sphere.

"It wasn't doing that before," Amira commented in awe. "There were rifts open in this room when we got here, but I closed them."

"I believe it's a map," Zan explained.

He touched a random point and a small sliver of shimmering light appeared before him. Amira slid her fingers across the sphere and widened the new rift slowly until it was about a foot in diameter.

"Well done," Zan praised her. "Now to find out where that is."

He pulled out a nav unit and stuck his hand through the rift to determine the coordinates.

"Goodness, this is over a million light years away!" He sounded delighted by the prospect.

He and Amira shifted the endpoint on the sphere until the view on the other side began to look familiar. They found the correct quadrant, then the correct planet, and then, finally, the *Aurora.*

"I'm sure there's a better way to do that, but it will do for now!"

I'd never seen Zan so animated.

Excitedly, Amira widened the rift.

A mix of crew members and refugees on the other side stood frozen, gaping at us in awe.

"Well, here goes nothing," Amira shrugged.

With the Gateway in hand, she stepped through before I could stop her.

She turned back to look at me with the biggest smile I'd ever seen, beckoning the others through.

Zan went next, followed by Mariella, then Tu'ver. I went last. I stepped through the shimmering rift.

It was cold, like being immersed under icy water. For a brief moment, I could see the endless galaxy spread out on either side of me before my foot touched down in front of the *Aurora.*

AMIRA

So many people, wanting to talk about so many things.

I was proud to have helped, that the mission was a success, that my useless studies weren't so useless after all...

But what I really wanted was to get far away from the excited crowd and scrub off the mess from the fight.

Maybe I wasn't so different from Jeneva after all.

While we were gone, Jeneva had had me reassigned to a different cabin a few doors down from where she and Vrehx now lived. It was larger than the one I was originally assigned, and it only had one bed.

Guess I would never know who my roommate would have been. I was excited that I wouldn't have to share a room now. It was the perfect set-up for late night visits from Dax.

When we arrived back at the *Aurora*, I wanted nothing more than to take a scalding hot shower before crawling into bed next to him.

Dax, however, had to fill out a mission report before he could do anything else. We promised that we'd catch up later.

As soon as I entered my new cabin, I made a beeline for the shower. I scrubbed my body until my skin felt shiny and new, every trace of the fight with the hybrids scrubbed away.

I toweled off, tugged on the first shirt I could get my hands on, and collapsed on top of the bed, with my hair still wet.

I didn't know how much time had passed when the sound of my cabin door opening woke me.

"Dax, is that you?" I mumbled into my pillow, still mostly asleep. "Come keep me warm."

I extended a hand and patted the space on the bed beside me. I was freezing. Served me right for not letting my hair dry all the way or taking the time to get under the covers.

"Dax?" A man hissed.

My eyes flew open, and I shot upward.

That wasn't Dax.

I grabbed at the covers and yanked them over my exposed legs before turning on the bedside light.

Ren stood in the doorway of my cabin, an angry gleam in his eyes.

"What the hell are you doing in my room?" I snapped.

He took a step forward, letting the door slide closed behind him.

"Why would you think an alien would come into your room?" he asked slowly.

I tightened my grip on the bed covers.

"I don't see how that's any of your business."

"It's my business when my friends start taking alien scumbags to bed!" Ren yelled.

I flinched.

"You need to leave. Right now," I demanded.

I wondered if there was anyone nearby who would hear me if I called for help.

Ren had clearly gone off the deep end.

"Not until I get what I came for."

The smile that appeared on his face made my stomach twist.

"You're not getting anything from me if you're going to talk about Dax like that," I insisted.

Ren wasn't very tall, but he was stocky.

I doubted that I could force him out of the room if it came to that.

"Did you fuck him for a nicer room?" he asked, looking around my relatively spacious cabin.

"I live in a shoebox now, with two others," he spat bitterly.

"Jeneva arranged for me to have this room," I explained. "She wanted me closer to her, closer to where I can be helpful. Maybe if you pulled your head out of your ass, you could be useful, too."

"I'd rather die before I do anything to help those aliens," he sneered.

"Keep that up, and you'll get your wish," I warned him. "The less prepared we are as a team, the easier it'll be for the Xathi to pick us apart."

"You think you know so much when you don't know anything at all," he scoffed.

"I know a hell of a lot more than you do," I replied.

"No, you don't. But there is one thing you know that I need to know."

He stepped farther into the room, closer to my bed.

My heart beating in my ears, I forced my limbs to stay still, not scramble for distance.

"What do you need to know?" I asked steadily, fingers clutching the covers to quiet them.

"I need to know what you found on your mission."

My surprise was clear on my face. "What?" I blurted. "Why do you need to know?"

All Ren did in response was to laugh. It was a

normal enough laugh at first, but then it turned loud and shrill.

"What the fuck is wrong with you?" I demanded.

"What the fuck is wrong with you?" he shouted back. "I've been working non-stop to secure our safety, and you betray me by taking up with one of them."

"I have no idea what you're talking about!" I cried. "What does that have to do with my expedition?"

"I cut us a deal." He was excited now, practically bouncing on the balls of his feet. "It was all lined up and perfect, but you ruined it. So, I made another deal. Somehow you managed to ruin that, too. But you can make it all better by telling me what you found!"

"You're not making any sense," I groaned.

I was worried that Ren had gone completely insane. Looking at him now, I couldn't believe he was ever my friend.

"What deal did you make?"

"You're not the only one who snuck off the *Vengeance*," he grinned. "You were just the only one to get caught."

"You left the *Vengeance*?" I didn't understand. "Why?"

"The Xathi scouts were so close to finding us anyway," he shrugged. "I thought I'd help them in exchange for a promise of safety."

The world tipped on its axis.

My chest ached as if I'd been dealt a blow from an iron fist.

"You...told the Xathi where the *Vengeance* was hidden?" I rasped.

"Yes," he said.

The idiot was proud.

"I was going to find you and get you off the ship, but you'd gone off with them."

"People died, Ren." I shook my head, still not fully believing his words. "Not just the aliens you hate, but humans. Your actions killed several humans."

"I was willing to pay for your life with theirs," he shrugged.

I was going to be sick.

"But it didn't matter. You weren't there. So, I had to make another deal. As soon as I heard you were going off on a mission to recover something, I promised the Xathi that knowledge."

"Why would you do that?" I asked.

"How can you ask that? Isn't it obvious?" Ren's eyes were bulging as he took another step forward. "It's for us. I did all of this so we can have a life together. The Xathi won't harm us if we give them the information they want! They'll leave us alone."

What a stupid, stupid man.

I took a slow, deep breath.

I wanted to freak out. I wanted to scream and throw

things at his thick skull, but right now, I needed to remain calm.

No. Actually, what I needed to do was get him somewhere that others could see.

"You'd do all that for me?" I asked, forcing my eyes wide, like some pathetic lovestruck teen.

"Yes!" His eyes lit up.

He thought I finally understood. "I'd do anything for you. That's why I need you to tell me what you found, so I can save you."

I felt a pang in my chest. The poor idiot probably believed he was doing the right thing.

Of course, the Xathi wouldn't spare him. He was nothing more than a pawn. They'd kill him as soon as they decided he was no longer useful.

"It's too complex to explain in words," I said, biting my lip and shaking my head slowly. "I don't fully understand it myself."

The anger returned to his eyes.

"However," I continued, "I can show you. Maybe you'll be able to learn enough to please the Xathi."

"It will have to be," he smiled.

He extended his hand to me.

"I need a moment to get dressed," I said, pulling the covers tighter around me.

"Time is of the essence, my love. What you're wearing won't matter soon."

He thrust his hand closer to me. I took it. I hated the way his clammy skin felt against mine, but I had to keep the illusion going until I could get help.

I stepped out from under the covers in only the shirt I'd grabbed when I got out of the shower and a pair of black underwear.

Ren's gaze roved over my bare legs.

I wanted to claw his eyes out.

Later, I promised myself.

We walked out of my cabin together to a totally empty hallway.

"Which way?" he asked, giving my hand a squeeze.

I thought I was going to throw up right then, but I steadied myself. I didn't know where Fen had put the Gateway. I assumed she had a safe place for it where it could be monitored and studied.

"This way," I said, and picked a direction at random.

We didn't see anyone as we got into an elevator to take us down to the lower levels of the *Aurora*. When we stepped out, there was a K'ver guard stationed nearby.

I recognized him, but I didn't know his name. He gave me an odd look when Ren and I approached.

Help me, I mouthed as we passed.

A long moment passed.

Another.

Would he be able to understand me, read my lips? Did the damn neurotransmitters even work that way?

I kicked myself for the millionth time for not learning more about them, for being so resistant to everything alien.

For being so stupid to let something so minor take me away from Dax.

A third step.

A fourth.

"Stop right there!" the K'ver barked.

Ren halted as relief washed over me.

"You don't have clearance to be down here."

"Can't two lovers take a stroll without being harassed?" Ren sneered.

"We aren't lovers," I yelled, trying to get away from Ren's grip. "He's a Xathi spy!"

Ren dropped my hand and tried to run, but he was no match for the speed and strength of the K'ver guard. Ren was on the ground in shock restraints in a matter of moments.

"She's a liar!" Ren shrieked, and wiggled against the guard's tight grip.

"Take him to General Rouhr immediately," I said, ignoring Ren. "He's the one who gave away the location of the *Vengeance*. He confessed to everything when he entered my cabin without permission."

"Thank you for bringing this to our attention," the guard nodded. Others had arrived. "We'll take it from here."

"She's lying!" Ren wailed, though the guards paid him no attention.

"The Urai will look into your mind and see the truth," one of them said.

All color drained from Ren's face.

"Do you need assistance, miss?" one of the guards asked. "Did he harm you?"

I turned away, legs like rubber, a bitter taste in my mouth.

All I wanted was Dax.

DAXION

I refused to let Amira out of my sight since that lunatic had gotten into her room.

Though she pretended otherwise, I knew the ordeal had shaken her.

I worried she blamed herself.

After all, Ren only went to that extreme because he claimed to love her.

That wasn't love.

That was obsession. Cowardice.

Stupidity and fear.

I'd offered to kill him, but Vrehx didn't seem to think I was volunteering for completely altruistic reasons.

General Rouhr called a meeting the day after Ren was taken into custody.

Amira and I walked together into one of the plush conference rooms aboard the *Aurora*.

As much as I hated to admit it, I'd been a little frustrated that the *Aurora* wasn't a military ship, scornful at all the luxury.

After spending a few nights down in the temple? I was glad for cushioned chairs and comfortable accommodations.

Amira and I sat side by side, hands clasped. I absentmindedly traced patterns over the back on her hand with my thumb.

Karzin, Sk'lar, and Vrehx were already present.

Jeneva was the next to arrive. She gave Amira a sisterly kiss on the top of her head before sliding into the seat next to her. This seemed to surprise Amira, but she remained silent.

She hadn't spoken much since the incident with Ren. But I could tell she was pleased Jeneva chose to sit next to her.

Zan and Fen arrived together and sat beside each other. The human doctor, Evie Parr hurried in as if she was worried she was late. She smiled at everyone before she sat down.

General Rouhr was the last to arrive. He walked in with Vidia. I didn't know her well, but she was an important figure in the human government system and the voice of the human refugees.

"I would like to start this meeting off on a positive note," General Rouhr announced. "The expedition to the far desert was a great success. I offer my congratulations and gratitude to you, Amira."

Amira beamed as murmurs of agreement rippled through the room. I gave her hand a gentle squeeze.

"I'm so proud," I heard Jeneva whispered.

I knew that would mean the world to Amira.

"The Gateway is a spectacular find," Rouhr went on. "It would have been disastrous in the hands of the Xathi. Fen, you've made sure it's secure?"

Fen nodded and placed her hand on her speech pad.

"The Gateway has allowed us to stabilize the rift the Xathi came through and we've harnessed that rift's power more efficiently," she explained. "As a result, the repairs of the *Aurora* are expected to be completed much sooner than anticipated."

"How so?" Karzin asked.

"Our fabricators draw a lot of power," Fen replied. "Now that we can harness the rift properly, we can operate them without having to sacrifice more important things like food generation or waste removal. These fabricators can pull useful components from almost any organic material. Now that we can use them, it's much easier to obtain materials for repairs."

Huh. Like my quiver. I'd need to talk to her. Maybe it was time for an upgrade.

I thought back to the battle in the cavern, Amira behind me.

Never again.

"Impressive," Karzin nodded.

"It opens rifts between one point in space and another, right?" Vidia spoke up.

Fen nodded once more.

Vidia turned to Rouhr with an excited gleam in her eyes. "That's perfect for quick and safe evacuations. We can remove people from harm's way before the Xathi even reach them."

"Indeed." Rouhr's voice was warm, but there was some hesitation in his eyes.

I wondered why.

"Now, unfortunately, we have to discuss less pleasant matters, such as the human informant, Ren."

Amira stiffened beside me. I ran my thumb over the back of her hand again to calm her.

"I completed my examinations this morning," Evie spoke. "I didn't find any signs of hybridism or evidence of the Xathi queen controlling his actions. I believe he was simply a scared man who was weak."

This wasn't what Amira wanted to hear. It would've been easier for her to bear if Ren wasn't responsible for his choices.

"I see," Rouhr said heavily. "That's unfortunate."

"How can we be sure none of the other refugees are

running off to the Xathi?" Sk'lar directed his question at Vidia.

"I've been doing my best to keep everyone's spirits up," she replied. "I talk to as many people as I can in a day and none of them have led me to suspect any aggression towards the crew."

"But people can lie," Karzin jumped in. "Ren did. So can others. We should make an example of him."

"You mean kill him, and use his death to inspire fear?" Amira spoke.

All eyes fell on her.

"Believe me when I say that won't achieve any good. I'm sure some of you remember how I was when I was first brought aboard the *Vengeance*. If anyone of the refugees has the mindset that I did, making an example of Ren will only inspire more anger and hatred. If anything, it'll make people more likely to believe the lies the Xathi will tell them."

"Well spoken," General Rouhr nodded in her direction. "No, the Xathi informant will remain in a secure cell guarded at all hours. Perhaps, he can be persuaded to tell us if there are others inclined to go to the Xathi."

"He cost us our ship," Karzin snarled. "I say we throw him to the Xathi, and let him see how far their kindness goes."

"We have to be better than our enemy if we are

going to win this war," General Rouhr said calmly. "Defeating the Xathi is only half the battle. The other half is ensuring we don't become monsters ourselves."

"Apologies," Karzin grunted and fell into a brooding silence.

"I have a bright spot of news," Evie said before another disagreement could arise. "My mission to Einhiv may have been mostly unsuccessful, but I learned a great deal about hybridism. Right now, Leena is in the lab analyzing my work. She believes I'm on the right track to discovering a cure."

"How close are you?" General Rouhr asked.

"Not very," Evie admitted. "But I've managed to narrow in on a few compounds that affect the cells corrupted by hybridism. A few days ago, I had nothing."

"Have you tried any naturally occurring substances?" Jeneva asked.

"Not yet," Evie replied. "I was actually going to ask you for your input."

"I'll stop by the lab this evening," Jeneva grinned.

"Well, I consider that cause for optimism," General Rouhr smiled. "I look forward to hearing your progress reports. If there's nothing else to discuss, I'd say we're finished here."

"General," Sk'lar spoke up before anyone rose from their seats. "Now that we have the ability to control rifts, will we be leaving this planet?"

A heavy silence fell over the room. I knew the question of leaving had been prominent in the minds of the crew.

I stole a glance at Amira. I didn't know if the *Aurora* would leave this planet or not, but I did know one thing. If the *Aurora* left, I would not be on it unless Amira was, too.

Now that she knew about the Aeryx ruins, I thought it unlikely that she'd want to leave this planet for a very long time, if at all.

I knew Tu'ver would never leave Mariella, either. Same went for Vrehx, Sakev, and Axtin. We'd been lucky enough to find our mates on this strange planet, despite the Xathi threat.

I couldn't imagine any of us would be willing to part with them. If the *Aurora* left Ankau, it would be missing some crew members.

"I'm not sure there's a straight answer I can give," Rouhr said. "There is still work to be done on the *Aurora*."

"The ship sustained heavy damage during the crash," Fen spoke up. "We can repair her to the best of our ability, but even with our sophisticated equipment, I cannot guarantee she'll ever be safe for space travel."

"Understood," Sk'lar nodded.

"I'll keep you all informed on the *Aurora*'s progress," Rouhr said. "Dismissed."

AMIRA

Fen stopped me before I left the conference room.

"Do you have a moment?" she asked.

I nodded and turned to Dax. "I'll meet up with you later," I smiled and kissed his cheek.

He looked uneasy. He'd been at my side since Ren revealed he was the Xathi informant, and I was grateful. Knowing Ren got into my room so easily made me feel sick every time I thought about it.

But I'd have to get out on my own sometime.

With a quick spin, he scooped me up and kissed me until my head spun. "Let me know if you need me." I touched my lips, still feeling him as he left.

"What's up?" I asked Fen, slowly pulling myself back together.

"I don't understand the question," she replied, giving me a quizzical look.

I couldn't help but laugh.

"Sorry, it's a human expression. It means what do you need?" I clarified.

"I have an offer for you," she said. "Come with me."

I followed her down a hallway I'd yet to explore. We didn't walk far before stopping at a set of pristine white double doors with two windows for viewing.

There was an identical door across the hallway. Through the windows, I saw Evie and Leena bent over lab equipment. Fen must be taking me to a lab of some sort.

The room she brought me into was pure white. White floors, white walls, white counters. I was afraid to touch anything for fear of dirtying it.

On the far wall were rows of mounted shelves containing objects in glass boxes. Each box had a small plaque that I assumed had a description of the item.

"This is where we store and analyze unique finds from our travels," Fen explained. "The Gateway, of course, is far too valuable and dangerous to be kept in an open lab. Here, as you can see, we have a small collection that managed to survive the crash."

"This place is incredible," I whispered.

"It's yours to use freely," Fen said.

"Oh, I didn't bring anything else back with me from

the temple other than the Gateway," I explained quickly.

"I know," Fen said. "But you will."

"What do you mean?" I asked, trying not to get too excited too soon.

Fen walked over to one of the desks and pressed a button recessed into the surface. On the empty wall in front of her, a large segment slid down to reveal a screen. The white surface of the desk shifted, revealing a control panel.

Fen pressed a few buttons and pulled up a satellite scan like the one we first used to locate the Aeryx ruins.

"The Aeryx temple is not the only thing hidden beneath the surface of your world," Fen explained. "Now that the *Aurora* repairs are underway, it is time to seek out creative resources to use to our advantage. The structures you see now are likely to contain something useful to us."

"Something else like the Gateway?" I gaped.

"No, nothing so powerful as that," Fen corrected. "Rare metals and other natural resources are likely to be found here. However, I cannot retrieve them myself and there are no others besides Zan who are qualified. You have proven yourself to be dedicated, resourceful, and relentless. Fine qualities to have in a time of war."

"Thank you," I stammered, unsure of how to process her words.

"You may choose your first assignment from the three ruins I've already located. Depending on what we need, I will alter the satellite searches."

Suddenly, it all clicked in my head.

"You want me to go?" I couldn't have said anything more stupid if I'd tried.

"Of course," Fen tilted her head. "Do you not wish to?"

"No! I mean, yes! I do. I want to do this." I was flustered. This was everything I'd ever dreamed about.

Other than jumping up and down making high-pitched noises, I couldn't imagine what words would adequately explain how much she was giving me.

"Excellent," Fen nodded. "I'll leave you to plan your expedition."

Fen strode out of the lab, leaving me alone with the most sophisticated equipment any archeologist in the history of archaeology had ever had the privilege to work with.

Just like that, I had a job.

I approached the control panel, ready to spend the night learning the Urai control system, but it looked like I wouldn't have to. Someone had already come through and labeled everything in my native tongue.

I wonder how long they'd been planning on offering this to me. The computer was programmed to switch between my language, the Urai language, and the languages of the *Vengeance* crew.

Fen was incredibly thorough in her preparation of the lab.

I studied the satellite images of the new ruins. One wasn't far from the Aeryx site. Upon closer inspection, the structures reminded me of the pyramids built by the ancient Egyptians of Earth.

The second set of ruins captured my attention completely. It was on the other side of the planet, nearly at the southernmost point of Ankau.

Naturally, it was covered in snow, but it wasn't like the expansive tundras of Earth. From what I could see on Fen's incredibly detailed satellite, it was a forest.

A frozen forest.

How cool was that?

I pulled up Fen's notes to see what resource could be found there. From the name alone, I couldn't make out what it was or even pronounce it, but Fen had made a note that whatever it was could strengthen a repaired hull. That was most certainly important.

My first expedition would be there.

There wasn't much information on that area in the Ankau colonists' data archives.

It was noted as inhabitable, but as a last resort.

We were pretty much at last resort now, even if this

situation was nothing the original colonists could have dreamed of.

The desk was stocked with empty data pads I could use to make notes. Fen had really thought of everything. I sat at my new desk and got to planning right away.

I was so absorbed in my work that I didn't notice someone enter the lab until I felt a tap on my shoulder.

I screamed and leaped to my feet, knocking things off my desk with a clatter.

"Shit!"

Jeneva looked as scared as I felt.

"You scared the life out of me!" I placed my hand over my heart and laughed.

My heartbeat was thrumming beneath my ribs.

"I'm sorry!" Jeneva laughed, too. "I knocked, I called your name, and you didn't even look up. Believe it or not, I was trying not to scare you."

"I'm not sure I believe that," I teased. "You really called my name?"

"Twice," Jeneva affirmed.

"Damn," I sighed. "How'd you know I'd be here?"

"At first, I didn't. I went to your room, to Dax's room, and to the new refugee area. No one had seen you since the meeting. I'd been looking for you for over an hour when Fen told me where to find you."

"Over an hour?" It didn't feel like I'd been here that

long. "Sorry about that. Do you want to go get something to eat?"

Jeneva looked at me in bewilderment.

"Amira, it's past midnight. Snipes has already gone to bed," she said.

"What?" I blurted.

I looked around for a clock, but there wasn't one in the lab that measured time the way humans did. I'd have to bring one in later.

"Yup. You've been in here for ages," Jeneva confirmed. "I came in because I wanted to talk to you about something."

I'd been waiting for this. She was going to lecture me about going on the expedition without saying goodbye. I thought that, since Jeneva was so nice and sat by me during the meeting earlier today, I'd dodged this tricky conversation.

I guess I hadn't, after all.

"I'm sorry I left without telling you," I said before she could start scolding me. "It wasn't a sisterly thing to do."

Jeneva looked surprised.

"Oh. Thank you, I appreciate that," she said with a confused smile. "It hurt a bit when I realized you'd left, but that wasn't what I came to talk to you about."

Now it was my turn to look surprised.

"Oh?"

"I actually came to apologize," she confessed. "I wasn't understanding when you said you needed time to move on from the past. My life came together so perfectly out of the blue. You came back into my life, I met Vrehx, I found meaningful work. I became so happy so quickly, and I wasn't seeing how unhappy you still were. I couldn't understand why you wouldn't just be happy. It was self-centered and short-sighted of me. I'm sorry."

"I forgive you for meeting the love of your life, I guess?" I joked.

Jeneva rolled her eyes and smiled.

"I know what you're trying to say. Thanks for saying it. Though now I understand what you mean. My life came together pretty perfectly faster than I ever expected."

"I'm glad."

She opened her arms and enveloped me in a hug. We stayed like that for a while before my stomach rumbling ruined the moment.

"Are you sure Snipes is asleep?" I asked. "He never sleeps."

"I'm pretty sure I saw him stumbling into his quarters," Jeneva confirmed. "I bet we can sneak into the kitchen, though."

She waggled her eyebrows.

"I'm in!" I laughed. "Just let me clean up."

"Are you planning another trip?" Jeneva asked, looking at the mess I'd made of my desk.

Data pads filled with notes and maps were covering the desk surface, and I'd knocked more to the floor when she'd startled me.

"I am," I replied. "Fen asked me to plan a few expeditions to recover rare resources for the *Aurora*."

"That's amazing!" Jeneva gasped. "Where are you going?"

"I decided to go to the frozen forest on the other side of the world," I explained. "I've done the research, now I just need to put together a team."

"Did you say frozen forest?" Jeneva asked.

"I did. And I could use someone with great knowledge of plants and their properties to help me," I grinned.

"You want me to come?" Jeneva couldn't hide her smile.

"Absolutely. I couldn't imagine going without you."

EPILOGUE

I was exhausted after a long day of work, but I couldn't be happier. I had a role, a place in the grand scheme of things, and I wouldn't trade it for the world.

Juggling a stack of datapads with notes for the possible mission, I wiggled enough of my hand free to get it on the palm reader and unlock the door.

As I steep through, someone moved in the shadows.

"It's just me, darling," Dax said quickly.

Relief bloomed under my breastbone. Someone must've told him that was a human term of endearment.

I liked it.

I'd never been anyone's darling before. I should ask him if there was a Valorni counterpart term.

"What are you doing here in the dark?" I asked.

Suddenly, the room was illuminated with a soft golden light.

Dax had brought in a small round table and covered it with a salvaged piece of canvas.

On the table was a bundle of jungle flowers and two covered dishes from the mess hall. Floating above the table was a ball of light made to mimic the flickering of a fire.

"What's all this?" I placed the datapads on the edge of the cluttered desk, blinking away a sudden rush of tears.

"I believe it's what you humans call a date," Dax grinned.

I crossed the room and threw my arms around his neck.

He squeezed me close before letting me step back to survey his work.

"Jeneva helped me with the blooms," he explained. "I wouldn't want to mistakenly poison you during what's meant to be a romantic evening."

"That'd put a damper on things, for sure," I laughed.

I wondered how long Jeneva had kept this a secret from me.

"Dare I ask what's under the plate covers?"

Dax pulled a chair out for me like a real gentleman.

When I was seated, he uncovered the dish in front of me.

"Pasta!" I cried.

It was my favorite food growing up. I couldn't remember the last time I'd eaten it.

"Jeneva must've told you."

"She did," Dax admitted.

"I can't believe they had it on board."

The pasta noodles looked mouthwatering. They were served in a creamy orange sauce I didn't recognize. Vegetables that grew nearby were mixed in amongst dark slices of meat.

"They didn't," Dax said with a wry smile. "Tu'ver and I figured out how to make it. He did most of the work, but I chopped the vegetables."

"You figured out how to make pasta for me?" I was truly touched.

"If I'd known pasta was all it took to win your heart, I would've spared myself the trouble of plundering dangerous ruins," he said wryly.

"That'll teach you to ask next time."

I took a bite. It was the best thing I'd ever tasted.

The sauce was rich and just a little bit spicy. The meat was tender and flavorful, but I couldn't put my finger on what it was.

"This is amazing. What kind of meat is this?"

Dax paused between bites.

"That's the thing," he began. "Tu'ver got the meat from Snipes, who's still getting a feel for the Urai's kitchen stock. He said he had no idea what it was, just that it was safe to eat and tasted great."

"Snipes thinks everything is tasty," I countered. "But I agree, it's delicious."

"So, now that you know I can provide you with excellent food, are you planning on sneaking off the *Aurora* anytime soon?"

Dax poured us each a glass of dark purple liquid I assumed was some sort of spirit.

"I'm happy to report I have no intention of sneaking off into the night."

I took a sip. The drink was unrecognizable but delicious.

"The *Aurora* is my home now. I regret not treating the *Vengeance* more like a home."

"She was a fine vessel," Dax nodded in agreement.

"Do you miss it?" I asked.

"I'd been with the *Vengeance* for years. I knew the ins and outs of that ship almost as well as Thribb did. She had personality, believe it or not. Even when we were crashing into this planet, she kept fighting for us," he explained.

"You loved the ship as if she were a person." I smiled into my glass.

I thought it was sweet.

He was sweet.

"A good ship like that is like a good friend. The *Vengeance* carried us through the Abyss and back, and then sheltered us when she couldn't carry us anymore. It hurt to abandon her the way we did." He looked down at his plate.

"She may not be lost forever." I reached across the table and laid my hand over his.

"No, but I hate the idea of the Xathi crawling through her and looting her for spare parts," Dax shuddered.

There was anger in his eyes, but he seemed to remember himself.

"I apologize. This night isn't supposed to be about what we've lost. We're meant to be celebrating what we've gained." His easy smile returned. "Besides, I quite like the *Aurora*. She's a fine ship."

"They've already begun repairs," I added. "From what I understand, there's a good chance she'll be able to fly again."

"That would be something," Dax agreed.

We ate in contented silence for a few moments. I polished off the last of my food before he did.

"What are you celebrating?" I asked.

"What?"

"You said we were here to celebrate," I grinned. "I asked you what you're celebrating."

Dax grinned and took a long sip of his drink.

"Let's see, shall we? Our successful mission, the good that will come of having the Gateway in our possession, and I'm celebrating the amazing woman that made it all happen."

A blush rose to my cheeks. "Those are all worth celebrating." I dabbed at my eyes.

When had I become so soft?

"I'm glad the mission was a success. The Gateway will be useful, no doubt about it. But even if we hadn't recovered it, I'd still be celebrating." I continued.

"Oh?" Dax lifted a brow.

"Yes. I'd still be celebrating the fact that I've found the person I want to stand beside through all of this. No matter what happens."

Dax's smile reached all the way up to his eyes. He reached across the table to take my hand in both of his.

"I love you more than I could ever express," he said softly.

"And I love you more than I ever thought I could love someone," I replied.

We sat perfectly still for a long while, doing nothing but gazing into each other's eyes and watching the false firelight dance across each other's skin.

"Did you enjoy your dinner?" Dax indicated my empty plate.

"That was the best meal I've ever had."

I already wished I had another plateful to devour, even though I felt full to bursting.

Dax beamed. "Anytime you want something, I'll recruit Tu'ver, and we'll make it happen," he promised. "I think he likes having an excuse to get back in the kitchen."

I dabbed at the corners of my mouth with a napkin and rose from my seat. Whatever I'd drunk made me feel airy and carefree.

I walked around the table and settled myself in Dax's lap, letting my head rest on his shoulder, and he wrapped his arms around me.

"Lucky for me that you're the perfect size for this," he said.

"Lucky for me you're a giant," I replied.

He pressed a kiss onto the top of my head.

I traced a finger over the woven fabric of his shirt.

"I saw that big stack of notes you brought in," he commented. "I take it that your work is going well?"

"Extremely," I replied. "I was actually going to ask you if you'd be up for another adventure soon."

"Another adventure?" he repeated. "You mean another foolhardy trip to a crumbling ruin?"

"Yup."

"Filled with trapdoors, secret passages, and a slew of other horrible things?"

"Most likely."

He leaned back and looked at me.

And then he smiled.

"There's nothing I'd rather do."

LETTER FROM ELIN

I know it's been a bit of a journey with Amira, but I hope you enjoyed seeing her grow!

Next up, General Rouhr meets his match. Keep reading for a sneak peak, and then come along for the adventure!

XOXO,

Elin

PLEASE DON'T FORGET TO LEAVE A REVIEW!

Readers rely on your opinions, and your review can help others decide on what books they read. Make sure your opinion is heard and leave a review where you purchased this book!

Don't miss a new release! You can sign up for release alerts at both Amazon and Bookbub:

bookbub.com/authors/elin-wyn

amazon.com/author/elinwyn

For a free short story, opportunities for advance review copies, release news and the occasional cat picture, please join the newsletter!

https://elinwynbooks.com/newsletter-signup/

And don't forget the Facebook group, where I post sneak peeks of chapters and covers!

https://www.facebook.com/groups/ElinWyn/

SNEAK PEEK: ROUHR

R ouhr

THE FIRST THING that hit me in the morning was a fresh stack of datapads.

I suspected that those who delivered reports strategically picked times they knew I wouldn't be in.

Perhaps I'd bring a cot into my office and sleep there from now on. It would save me the time of walking back and forth to my cabin and force the shy datapad deliverers to face me.

I shook the thought away and picked up the first datapad in the new stack. No surprise, it was from Thribb, as was the one underneath it. A quick glance told me they contained much of the same information as the one he'd dropped off in the late hours of last night.

I valued Thribb's council, as well as the information he brought to my attention, but this was becoming excessive.

Time for something else.

The next contained a report from one of the evening guards who witnessed a small skirmish between two of the human refugees.

One stole the blanket of another, despite the fact she already had one of her own. An argument ensued, but the guard dispersed it, and the blanket was returned to its rightful owner.

That was something I'd noticed about humans. In times of crisis, they either banded together in a terrific show of support or turned on each other completely.

I was glad that the majority of the humans I'd met fell into the former category rather than the latter, though naturally there were a few exceptions.

As the unofficial leader of the refugees, I was sure Vidia Birch received a copy of this. She'd held a position of power in one of the first towns attacked by the Xathi, and the humans respected her.

Early on, we agreed that she'd handle the majority of the disciplinary actions in regard to the humans. It took a significant weight off my shoulders. It was only for serious offenses that I became involved, as it had been with Ren, the human Xathi informant.

I picked up the next in the stack.

Skrell.

Urai surveillance had shown that the Xathi mother ship was undergoing repairs. The damage that had been inflicted on it from its crash landing on the planet, as well as the battle that we had waged when killing the sub-queen, was in the process of being repaired.

Based on satellite photos, Fen and her team calculated that the Xathi ship would be spaceworthy in ten days.

When that happened, the slight advantage we had at this point over the Xathi would vanish.

The next report from the human doctor, Evie Parr, was far more hopeful. She was working on developing a cure to reverse the effects of hybridism.

The Xathi had infected the minds of a shockingly high number of humans, more than we'd ever seen before. The more control the Xathi held of the infected, the more Xathi-like they became.

Up until recently, we'd believed this was an irreversible condition.

Evie had been working practically around the clock since I'd sent her on a mission to the human city of Einhiv to study the condition.

The mission itself wasn't much of a success. Evie

almost succumbed to hybridism in the process, but managed to escape it.

But not long ago, Evie had found a selection of naturally occurring chemicals in the brain that, when combined with certain chemical agents, affected the spread of hybridism. The datapad she left for me didn't contain news of a major breakthrough, as I'd hoped, just the details of a few small steps in the right direction.

I tried to keep my hopes realistic.

The Urai lab was more advanced than ours on the *Vengeance*, but even its resources were limited. I hoped Evie could find what she needed to solve this puzzle.

And now, there was no more avoiding it.

Time for Thribb.

Head Engineer Thribb was tasked with keeping me abreast of the *Aurora's* repair progress.

At present, the top priority was repairing the significant damage done to the *Aurora's* hull. It was almost completely split open on one side when the ship crash landed on the planet's surface after falling through a rift in space, a rift my men, and myself by extension, were responsible for creating.

Fen had also provided me with updates about the quickly improving structural integrity of the ship. Progress had nearly tripled since an ancient space-travel device known as the Gateway was found and recovered by a small team of humans, my men, and a Urai scientist.

The Gateway was able to stabilize the rift, and the Urai were able to funnel more power to the *Aurora*. Now, the whole of the Urai's advanced technology was available to be used for repairs.

Thribb, however, had an ever-increasing list of other concerns, which he vocalized often. While he was pleased with the *Aurora's* progress, he now spent an inordinate amount of time calculating what would be required to make the ship efficient and safe for long-term space travel.

He, and a number of others, desired to leave the planet as soon as possible.

I understood their reasoning for that. According to his reports, available resources onboard were stretched thin between the humans and the crew. If we took on any more refugees, there would be even less to go around.

Still, there were camps of humans fleeing from the Xathi. Thribb knew I had every intention of opening up the *Aurora* to them if we found them, or if they found us.

Which brought up another of Thribb's many concerns: weight. When, or if, the *Aurora* was ready to

fly again, the less weight she carried, the easier her
journey would be.

Once, he had been bold enough to suggest that we
dismiss any human that wasn't working toward the
Aurora's repairs, but he received an instant reprimand
from me.

The humans on this ship would be allowed to stay
on this ship if they so chose, regardless of whether or
not the *Aurora* ever flew again, regardless of their
'usefulness' to the mission.

And none of this addressed my growing concern: it
didn't matter how many times I explained to Thribb
that we didn't know if the *Aurora* would ever be fit for
space travel again, he had convinced himself that she
would be.

Ordinarily, I wouldn't tolerate it, but it seemed to be
the only thing keeping Thribb going. Hope was
harmless enough, and I wouldn't take that away
from him.

Eventually, if his hopes were fulfilled, I'd have to
make the choice of leaving this planet or staying on to
help the humans.

The numbers all indicated that leaving was the most
logical thing to do, but if it came down to it, could I
bring myself to abandon the humans to the Xathi?

"General." A soldier appeared in the doorway to my

office, a tinge of worry in his voice despite the ramrod posture.

"Is something the matter?" I set the datapad down.

"Xathi are approaching the *Aurora* from the south, sir."

"How many?"

"Less than ten, but they have a mass of hybrids with them. I couldn't get a clear count."

"Is the barrier holding?" Thus far, the sonic barrier surrounding the *Aurora* had yet to be extensively tested.

Recently perfected and tested in a few small-scale skirmishes with the Xathi and hybrids, the barrier projected the same frequency as our neurogrenades, only it was much stronger.

With the help of the Urai, we were able to perfect the technology that ensured a barrier of safety around the *Aurora*. The grenades were strong enough to disrupt a Xathi individual's connection to the hive-mind and the queen, causing some to roam aimlessly, others to spasm and collapse.

This was a variation of the barrier the *Aurora* had once used in space. Now it was a combination of the technology the *Vengeance* crew had devised, that the humans had added their expertise to, and the Urai had provided the missing link for—a true model of interspecies coordination and cooperation.

It had the ability to give us yet another advantage in our conflict with the Xathi.

In its first real test, I was curious to see how the barrier held up.

"Last I saw, the Xathi were still examining the barrier from a distance. It's possible they can sense the barrier," he reported.

"Mobilize ground teams A and C in front of where the Xathi were gathering." I ran over the rest of my schedule mentally.

Skrell it.

"I'll join you shortly."

The soldier nodded and walked away briskly.

In one of my larger desk drawers, I kept a blaster and a tactical vest. I tugged the vest on and strapped the blaster to my hip. If necessary, I could borrow a more powerful weapon from the one of the ground teams.

I hurried outside, expecting to be rushing into a firefight, but when I arrived, very little was happening.

"Report." I nodded to the leader of ground team A. He was a Valorni, as were the majority of the soldiers that made up the ground teams. Their superior strength made them ideal for hand-to-hand combat.

The leader pointed out that the Xathi were as close as they could get to the widest part of the tear in the hull.

"Only a few hybrids have attempted to cross the barrier, General. But none have been successful. It's killed some, but that doesn't appear to deter the others. The Xathi won't get close to it. I think they know what it will do to them."

"Odd. If they know they can't get through, then why bother?"

"Who can say?" the soldier shrugged.

"Perhaps it's about the Gateway," I mused. "Enough hybrids saw Daxion and Amira with it, the queen must be able to assume it's here. That might make a renewed attack worth the resources to her."

"Makes sense to me." He resumed his tense watch, waiting for a break in the pattern.

Another hybrid approached the barrier, this one so overgrown with crystals that it was hard to tell it was once human. My mind wandered to Evie and her cure.

Seeing that wretched creature before me diminished my hope that anything could be done for it.

Though the barrier itself was all but invisible, aside from the tall metal spikes that transmitted the sonic frequency, I could tell exactly when the hybrid came into contact with it. Its body went rigid, and it looked like it was trying to remove its head from its body. Eventually, it skittered backward, much to the displeasure of the observing Xathi.

"What should we do, General?"

After what I'd seen, I wasn't concerned about the Xathi getting through the sonic barrier, but they would make trouble when we eventually needed to go beyond the safety of the *Aurora*.

If a small team needed to deploy on a scouting mission, the Xathi would know exactly how many were in the team and where they were going.

If more joined the mob that had already gathered around the *Aurora*, we risked becoming trapped.

"Mobilize the strike teams. Tell them to load minimal ammo and see if they can clear this mess away." I gestured to the small mob of hybrids and Xathi. "Ground team A can return to their usual duties." The soldier nodded once and departed.

Thribb had been particularly up in arms about ammo conservation. I agreed that we did need to use it sparingly until we could craft suitable replacements, but driving off a mob certainly qualified as a just reason.

A figure appeared in the corner of my eye. I tried not to wince as he approached.

"General, a word?" Thribb appeared at my side.

I forced a smile and nodded for him to speak.

"I've been running calculations—"

"As always." Thribb laughed uncomfortably as I cut in.

"Yes, General. As always. I'm sure you know what I'm going to say."

"That it's imperative we vacate the planet as soon as possible?"

"Exactly." Thribb nodded. "The thing is, General, I don't believe you understand how dire our situation is becoming. I mean no disrespect."

"Yet, you've managed it." I tried to keep my irritability in check. Thribb's people weren't big on social nuances. But this obsession of his was getting out of hand.

"Apologies. I've been allowed access to the Urai's interstellar maps. They're remarkably extensive. This is the first time I've gotten a clear picture of exactly where we are in the known universe. We are impossibly far from our home galaxy. The nearest planet suitable for landing will take a considerable amount of time for us to reach. We must start soon."

"How are you planning for us to make it home?" There was something terribly wrong with his reasoning, but he couldn't see it. "Or are you planning to use the Gateway?"

"We must leave immediately if we are to have any hope at all," he insisted. "The Gateway is still untested." He scowled. "Even if it does work, it only eliminates the concern for traveling distances. The Gateway cannot generate food, assist in emergency repairs, or maintain suitable oxygen levels and cabin pressure. We have what we need to maintain those things now, but the longer we linger on this planet, the less we will have when it comes time to leave."

"Yes, I believe you've told me that before." I tried not to grit my teeth.

"Then why haven't you—"

"Then why haven't I what? Abandoned the planet? Abandoned a civilian population to whom we've brought a war? You insist that I don't understand, but I suspect it is you, Thribb, who doesn't understand. I know little of your people, but I cannot imagine them all to be as unfeeling as you have shown me you can be."

"It's my job to assure that our vessel, whichever vessel that may be, is fit for space travel and assure the safety of those on board. Your unwillingness to face reality," he waved his datapad which contained his multitude of calculations, "has made my job very difficult as of late."

"You're out of line." I never raised my voice when I was angry, but Thribb knew my temper was reaching its snapping point.

At least he had the decency to step back, even if he kept chattering. "It would go against my conscience to stay silent when you are putting the crew at serious risk. I believe you've become too emotionally invested, and that has marred your ability to make rational decisions, despite the overwhelming evidence that immediate evacuation is the only choice."

"You're dismissed, Thribb. Don't come to me again unless you've obtained new information."

"But, General—"

"Dismissed!"

Thribb left without another word.

I stood behind my men and watched the hybrids continuously try to move through the sonic barrier.

As much as I tried to put it out of my mind for the time being, there was something Thribb had said that stuck with me.

Many that I'd served under in the past preferred to leave their emotions out of the equation.

They claimed it made making difficult choices much easier.

Up until now, I'd strongly disagreed.

I believed becoming emotionally invested allowed the right decision to shine through more clearly.

However, this wasn't just a difficult decision—this was an impossible decision. I had to consider the fact that Thribb might have a point.

Perhaps this was a decision that needed to be made only with logic.

. . .

Get Rouhr Now!

https://elinwynbooks.com/conquered-world-alien-romance/

VIDIA

Between wrangling minor disputes between refugees, assigning quarters, and attempting to help locate missing family members from the Xathi attacks, lately I'd spent every moment of any spare time in the labs with Evie.

General Rouhr had said he'd give us as much time as possible to find a cure for the hybrids, but we all knew the clock was ticking.

Medical science and chemistry weren't my strong suits, so I'd enlisted Leena to assist Evie. With both of their capable hands, it was easier to run tests and analyze data, and I could wash bottles, carry, and fetch.

Anything to help.

Already, Leena had a few ideas. I didn't understand much of the technical talk, but essentially, Leena had a list of adjustments she could make to the synthetic chemicals she'd created to make them more efficient and effective than the naturally occurring brain chemicals Evie was experimenting with.

Evie and Leena made a fantastic team. They'd

shared a lab on the *Vengeance* and were already accustomed to working with each other.

On Fen's recommendation, I'd brought in a Urai scientist named Glint, who had conducted several in-depth studies on the Xathi before landing on our planet.

Glint wasn't one for conversation, but from the excited chatter of Evie and Leena, she knew what she was doing and had filled in a missing piece of the puzzle.

At the moment, she was creating simulations on what a hybrid's brain chemistry looked like in various stages of infection. Once those simulations were complete, Leena and Evie could test their work.

The trio worked in harmony while I sat off to the side fidgeting, wishing there was more I could do.

"So, how long until we have a cure?" It'd been hours, at least, since I'd asked.

Evie sighed heavily and glared at me.

"If you ask me that one more time, I'm banning you from the lab. You know full well that this sort of thing doesn't run on a schedule. I could have a breakthrough in five minutes or five months."

I understood her testiness. There was a lot resting on her shoulders now.

"I know, I know." I put my hands up in surrender.

"It's actually not a bad thing that the hybrids keep flinging themselves at the sonic barrier, you know," Leena commented mildly. "Certainly, doesn't hurt that we have a steady supply of samples for testing."

"Leena," Evie gasped.

The chemist just shrugged. "You know I'm right. We can't work blind, and being soft-hearted isn't going to solve anything."

I could see that Evie didn't like it, but we all knew the truth. We needed every advantage we could possibly get, even if it was a tad... grisly.

"I don't understand why they're doing it, though," Leena added. "You'd think after they saw one die, they'd stop."

"I don't think they can control it." Evie would know better than any of us. Not long ago, she'd nearly lost her mind to the Xathi queen.

It still boggled my mind. "Then why would the Xathi queen force them into a barrier that would kill them? She must have realized she can't get to us."

"Maybe they're a distraction? She could be planning something bigger."

I agreed. "Still doesn't seem very logical."

"They're giant crystal bugs hell-bent on wiping out our population. Why are you looking for logic?" Leena gave a dry laugh.

"Because they're supposed to be military geniuses, too," I replied.

Evie amended that it could be a psychological thing. "She tried to manipulate me when she was in my head. She knows we know that the hybrids were once humans. Maybe she's just being spiteful by forcing so many to die in front of us."

"That's horrible." I shuddered.

"Hey, Leena! Come look at this." Evie was peering through a microscope.

Despite the topic of conversation, a smile bloomed over her features.

I took that as a good sign. Leena abandoned her work and peered through the microscope, too.

"That's great!" A smile appeared on her face, as well.

"What's great?" I didn't want to look through the microscope. I wouldn't understand what I was seeing.

"Hold on." Evie's excitement was growing by the second.

She gestured to Glint, who wasn't fond of using the speech-pad to talk, and asked her to look into the microscope, too. Glint silently analyzed whatever she was seeing. When she pulled away after a few minutes, she nodded at Leena and Evie with approval.

If she had a mouth, I guessed she'd be smiling.

"What is it?" I couldn't contain my curiosity. "Did you find a cure?"

"Not yet," Evie cautioned me. "But we're finally seeing the reaction we've been looking for. I think we've found the right combination of chemicals."

"So, what does that mean?" I asked.

Leena chimed in to explain that we needed to find the correct proportions. "We believe the Xathi queen alters the brain chemistry of a subject until it's shifted to a state that's compatible with hers. Once it's compatible, somehow she's able to take control, not only mentally, but by changing the body's physiology." She drummed her fingers on the workbench. "I'm not sure if we'll ever know exactly how she does that. But now, we have the correct mixture of natural and synthetic chemicals, so it could be possible for us to reverse the queen's damage."

"And that all means..." I prompted.

"We can potentially kick the Xathi queen out of someone's brain," Evie clarified.

"Incredible!" I clapped my hands together. "And you're sure?"

Leena opened her mouth, no doubt to launch into another lengthy and technical explanation, but Evie cut in.

"Yes, we're sure." she grinned.

I couldn't wait to inform General Rouhr. I so hoped he'd be pleased. Like everyone else, I heard the swirl of rumor and worry that floated through the ship. I knew that soon he'd have to make some decisions. Hard ones.

Hopefully, this bit of good news would be enough to buy us more time, maybe give him some leverage. "Excellent work, ladies. I'll check in later."

I rushed out of the lab, excitement bubbling under my skin. Evie was so close. A cure could be days, maybe even hours, away.

Rouhr's office was empty when I checked for him, so I asked one of the guards stationed nearby. He wasn't on the *Aurora* at all, but on the ground outside. I thought that was strange, but I needed to speak with him immediately.

I took the elevator down to what we'd all started calling the ground floor. It wasn't the main hub of the *Aurora*, but it was where the tear in the hull lead right out to the ground.

I stepped back in surprise when I stepped out of the elevator. More than half of the rip in the hull was sealed up and in its final stages of repair.

At this rate, we'd need a new name for the level. I figured it wouldn't be long until the hull was completely finished and they could move on to repairing the engines and thrusters.

"General?" There were several soldiers stationed in front of the tear in the hull. They'd brought out storage crates to use as barricades, though they weren't taking any fire. Their guns and blasters, on the other hand, were aimed at the invisible wall that was the sonic barrier.

On the other side, I could see a large gathering of Xathi and hybrids. The Xathi still held back, while the hybrids charged right into the barrier. The frequency of the sonic barrier was calibrated to deter full Xathi.

I could only imagine what it was doing to the weaker hybrids, day after day. The sonic barrier didn't kill them right away, but that didn't stop the hybrids from running into it over and over.

Occasionally, one was strong enough to fight through the disruptive wavelengths. The soldiers immediately shot it down.

General Rouhr stood behind his men, surveying the damage.

"Wouldn't it be kinder to shoot them before they encounter the sonic barrier?" I couldn't help but ask.

"Kinder, perhaps," he nodded, eyes still fixed on the attackers. "But I'd rather watch and see if they learn to stop trying. Besides," his lips twisted into a half-smile, "we need to conserve ammo."

My shoulders slumped. "Evie thinks they don't have any control over their bodies."

"I'm inclined to agree with her. When they're exposed to those sonic wavelengths, they're essentially rattling their own brains."

I could've been mistaken, but I thought I detected pity in his voice.

"I've got some news that might cheer you up." I smiled. "Evie, Leena, and Glint have made an astounding breakthrough. A cure isn't far off."

"That's terrific." Rouhr's dark eyes glinted. "How long?"

"Evie almost threw me out for asking that question," I playfully warned Rouhr. "She can't give a timeline. It doesn't work that way. But it's only a matter of time."

The warmth drained from Rouhr's eyes. "Everything is a matter of time." There was a barrage of blaster fire as another hybrid managed to get past the barrier, though it was already falling before the first blast struck it. "I've made a decision."

"What's that?" Dread pooled in my stomach.

"As soon as the *Aurora* is flight-ready, my men and I are leaving." At least Rouhr had the courage to look me in the eyes when he told me. I'd give him that, but that's all I was going to give him.

"You can't be serious." I laughed, though nothing was funny. "I've just told you how close we are to finding a cure, and you tell me you're abandoning us?" Rage shot through my veins, white-hot and searing.

"I have to start thinking realistically." Rouhr's voice sounded infuriatingly calm and even. "I want to give you as much time as I can. But you said so yourself,

Evie can't tell us when she'll have a cure. Thribb has told me when the *Aurora's* repairs will be complete, and I know how long we can sustain ourselves this way. We can't wait indefinitely for a cure that might not come in time."

"I'm not asking for you to wait indefinitely." My voice was rising. "I'm asking you to think about what your decision means for us."

"Night after night, it's kept me awake."

"Poor thing, I've been awake night after night, too, because the fate of my race was in the hands of someone else."

Rouhr opened his mouth to speak, but I cut in anyway, too angry to care about interrupting a general. An alien. Whatever.

"Do you realize what happens when you leave? Evie loses her lab. She loses every chance of finding a cure. Hundreds of people lose their food, shelter, and protection."

"I've offered the shelter of the *Aurora* indefinitely. That includes when we leave this planet."

"So that's the only choice we get? Abandon our home or die? And what of the thousands that aren't on the *Aurora*? Don't they matter?"

"I have to think about my men." Rouhr's calm tone was cracking. "My men are trapped here while the

Xathi are ravaging their homeworlds, too. Don't you think they deserve a say in where they go?"

That did it. I snapped.

"You're paying for your worlds with mine. There's a chance to save thousands and thousands of lives, and you're choosing not to take it. Justify it however you want, but that's the truth of the matter. Now, please excuse me."

I stormed away, leaving Rouhr standing among his soldiers with a scowl on his face and sadness in his eyes.

ROUHR

I hadn't slept in two days. Vidia's words echoed in my mind every moment of every day since we'd last spoken.

She was right.

I had allowed myself to mistake the logical decision for the right decision when I knew that, oftentimes, it was never that simple.

Vidia hadn't spoken more than a few sentences to me since I informed her of my decision, which wasn't surprising. We still had to interact often, since our jobs overlapped so much, but she avoided me as much as possible.

I knew how much she believed I'd do the right thing.

She'd put her faith in me, and I let her down.

I couldn't pin down why the thought bothered me so much, besides the obvious reason. It wasn't just that I'd be letting the humans down—it was that I'd be letting her down.

This was a war. War required sacrifices and difficult choices. I'd made a wrong choice, and if I could find a way to amend it, I would.

Vidia said there was always something to be done. I just needed to find something more substantial than a cure that might never come.

"General!"

I turned my head sharply toward the soldier who had called my attention. I could tell by his tone that it wasn't the first time he'd called me.

"Speak." I nodded.

"More Xathi and hybrids are arriving at the barriers. The strike teams have docked to restock their ammo."

"They're in the docking bay now?" The soldier nodded. "Tell them to come to the main conference room immediately, but only if you think the ground soldiers can handle the Xathi."

He confirmed that they could. "Hardly any actually make it through the sonic barrier. The Xathi don't even try. It's just the hybrids."

I paused, processing his statement. It suddenly made sense.

"Call out the snipers to join the ground crew, except for Tu'ver. But I'll send him out after the strike team meeting. Replace the entire ground team with snipers if you can."

"Sir?" the soldier confirmed.

"The Xathi aren't trying to attack. They're just trying to get us to waste our ammo. Snipers will take out the hybrids in one shot. Make sure they know to conserve as much as possible." The soldier nodded his head once and walked away.

I made my way to the larger conference room one deck up. It didn't take long for my crew to arrive.

They looked confused. I'm sure they were wondering why I'd pulled them from combat. It was strange to think that the Xathi were so close to us, but couldn't reach us.

Once everyone I'd asked for was present, I spoke.

"I formed your strike teams long ago as a way to reward the best and brightest of my soldiers and to make sure superior forces could be sent where they were needed most. Today, I've called you in for a different and somewhat unusual reason."

"Is this about the *Aurora* repairs?" Vrehx asked.

"It is." I nodded. "Thribb and I have been meeting regularly for some time now, as I'm sure you all know."

"We know Thribb wants to leave," Sakev scoffed. "Can't think about anything else."

"And you don't?" Karzin shot back.

Sakev was going to say something back, but I cleared my throat. All attention was drawn back to me.

I ran my ship differently than most other generals. My crew didn't need permission to speak. They were free to voice their thoughts.

I believed that, because of that, the respect my crew had for me was genuine. I didn't demand respect, then punish them when it was withheld. I sought to earn it. I believed it made all the difference.

But this was still my meeting, and it would run to my time.

"Thribb continuously runs calculations, measuring everything from ammunition to refugee resources. Finding the Urai and saving the *Aurora* was a stroke of luck. It's much better equipped to house refugees than the *Vengeance* was. What it lacks in defense weaponry, it makes up for in its technology, like the sonic barriers."

"General, you're not saying you prefer this luxury cruise liner to the *Vengeance*, are you?" Sk'lar lifted a brow.

I gave a short chuckle.

"I wouldn't go that far," I replied. "The *Vengeance* was designed to fight the Xathi. That's what we need. However, I think we all know the *Vengeance* isn't likely to fly again. The *Aurora*, on the other hand, has a much better chance."

"The hull is nearly repaired," Axtin interjected. He'd been one of the first to see the *Aurora* when she crashlanded. "But do you think she'll fly again? That's two entirely different things."

"From the reports, I have high hopes," I answered honestly. The repairs were going more smoothly than I would've guessed.

"So, is that it, then?" Rokul spoke up. "The *Aurora* will likely fly again, and when she does, we can finally pack up and get back to the real fight."

"This *is* a real fight," Tu'ver said through gritted teeth.

"This is one Xathi ship targeting a small civilian population. Back in our galaxy, there are hundreds of ships ravaging our worlds as we speak—our homes, remember? I'd consider that a higher priority," Rokul shot back.

At this point, I took a step back and listened. This was the sort of open discussion I'd been hoping to elicit. This was when I learned the most about the crew.

If things got out of hand, I'd step in. But these unfiltered discussions were more informative than anything else.

"It's our fault the Xathi are here. It's our responsibility to deal with them," Vrehx remarked.

"It's *your* fault," Karzin emphasized. "It was on your order that an experimental weapon was fired, tore a hole in the universe, and brought us here, away from the real war."

Vrehx's eyes were murderous, but he knew better than to resort to violence.

"It doesn't matter whose fault it is," Sk'lar argued. "We're not going to abandon a civilian population to the Xathi. It's against everything we stand for."

"I joined up to protect *my* people on *my* world," Rokul interjected. "I have sisters and a mother that need my protection, and I'm no good to them if I'm stuck here." His brother, Takar, echoed his sentiments.

Axtin rolled his eyes upon hearing this. "We all have families to worry about."

"Not all of us," Sakev muttered.

But Karzin wasn't one who would easily back down. "Just because some of you don't have anything to go back to, it doesn't mean I want to trade the lives of my family for the lives of these humans, galaxies away from home."

"Enough." I raised one hand. The crew went silent, though I could still feel their anger radiating off them. "It would seem that you have some mixed feelings on the subject of leaving. Not a surprise. Let's turn the discussion to solving a problem, rather than arguing about it."

"What's there to solve? This isn't our planet. This isn't our problem," Karzin stubbornly insisted.

Whether or not I agreed, I did understand his frustration.

Some of the crew knew for a fact that their loved ones had been killed in the initial Xathi attacks on our respective worlds.

Karzin was one of many who didn't know if his family was alive or not, which was arguably worse.

I hadn't been able to receive any reports from other units concerning the state of our home planets before we fell through the rip, but I remember when the Xathi first appeared.

They were quick to kill and destroy.

On my planet, they knew exactly where to strike to hurt us the most. I'm sure it was the same for the other planets.

I wouldn't dare say this out loud. I hated to even think it.

But if we did return to our homeworlds, I doubted there would be much left to return *to*.

"Even if the *Aurora* is ever declared fit for space travel," Tu'ver spoke over Karzin, "I can tell you now, I won't be on it. I'll be staying here. I'll fight for the humans, regardless."

"As will I," Vrehx seconded.

Nearly half of the strike teams declared they would

willingly stay behind even if the *Aurora* was cleared for space travel. There was a clear trend. All who agreed to stay had grown close to the humans while they were here, joined by many of those who knew they had no family back home to defend.

It was no secret that some of my crew had found love in the arms of human women. Many had also built strong friendships.

Those who were adamant about leaving hadn't socialized much with the humans. They'd likely avoided contact on purpose, knowing we'd have to leave at some point.

This divide presented a whole new slew of problems. If the *Aurora* left Ankau, it would be leaving without many vital crewmembers.

I'd need Thribb to factor that into his unending calculations. He'd probably be thrilled at the challenge.

"What of the cure for hybridism?" Daxion spoke up. "How does that change things?"

"It's progressing," I replied. "Not as quickly as I'd like, but there's nothing to be done about that."

"Evie's working night and day to make it happen," Sakev growled. "She doesn't rest, even when I tell her to."

"I know she is," I agreed. "It's simply a matter of time. A cure needs to be produced before we leave on the *Aurora*."

"So, the *Aurora* will leave, if she's able?" Karzin insisted.

"As of this moment, that's in our best interest," I announced. "However, the development of a cure could change or forestall that."

"That'd be even more of a reason to leave," Rokul said. "If they can cure the hybridism, the humans will have more people available to fight against the Xathi. They won't need us."

"That's not for you to decide," I corrected. "I've given you all of the information I have at present. You're all dismissed, but let me warn you now," I added before they could slip off, "should I hear of any arguing or similar conduct over today's discussion outside of this room, there will be consequences." I didn't lift my gaze until I received a nod of understanding from everyone.

When they'd all gone, I lowered myself into the closest seat.

I enjoyed meeting regularly with the crew. These meetings usually provided a sense of clarity.

But now I had just confirmed that the crew was as torn about this as I was.

A headache pulsed at my temple.

Of all things, I was craving the humans' coffee.

And maybe a sympathetic ear to share it with. But

Vidia still wasn't talking to me, so coffee alone it would be.

GET ROUHR NOW!

https://elinwynbooks.com/conquered-world-alien-romance/

DON'T MISS THE STAR BREED!

Given: Star Breed Book One

When a renegade thief and a genetically enhanced mercenary collide, space gets a whole lot hotter!

Thief Kara Shimsi has learned three lessons well - keep her head down, her fingers light, and her tithes to the syndicate paid on time.

But now a failed heist has earned her a death sentence - a one-way ticket to the toxic Waste outside the dome. Her only chance is a deal with the syndicate's most ruthless enforcer, a wolfish mountain of genetically-modified muscle named Davien.

The thought makes her body tingle with dread-or is it heat?

Mercenary Davien has one focus: do whatever is necessary to get the credits to get off this backwater mining colony and back into space. The last thing he wants is a smart-mouthed thief - even if she does have the clue he needs to hunt down whoever attacked the floating lab he and his created brothers called home.

Caring is a liability. Desire is a commodity. And love could get you killed.

https://elinwynbooks.com/star-breed/

ABOUT THE AUTHOR

I love old movies – *To Catch a Thief, Notorious, All About Eve* — and anything with Katherine Hepburn in it. Clever, elegant people doing clever, elegant things.

I'm a hopeless romantic.

And I love science fiction and the promise of space.

So it makes perfect sense to me to try to merge all of those loves into a new science fiction world, where dashing heroes and lovely ladies have adventures, get into trouble, and find their true love in the stars!